Hen's Teeth: Short Stories from the Bird Brain Books

The Bird Brain Books, Volume 4

Autumn Mist

Published by Autumn Mist, 2023.

This is a work of fiction. Similarities to real people, places, or events are entirely coincidental.

HEN'S TEETH: SHORT STORIES FROM THE BIRD BRAIN BOOKS

First edition. February 15, 2023.

Copyright © 2023 Autumn Mist.

ISBN: 979-8215050668

Written by Autumn Mist.

Also by Autumn Mist

The Bird Brain Books
This One's for the Birds
Carry On: Death Doulas of the Apocalypse
Unhatched Be: The Rise of Steampunk Portland
Hen's Teeth: Short Stories from the Bird Brain Books

Watch for more at www.autumnmistlit.com.

Table of Contents

This book is dedicated to my siblings. I could not ask for more perfect companions on this journey through life.

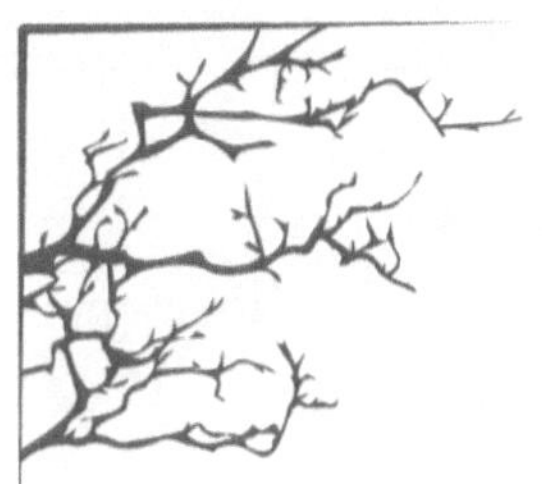

Spark

I'm from a family of warriors with a different way of living. I was always proud of my dad for the years he served in the military, but it also made him distant and sometimes unpredictable.

I spent a big part of my childhood just waiting for Dad to come home, and then when he did, he wasn't the dad I remembered. The true mark of the warrior is pain, and my dad came back hurting. His heart hurt so he yelled at my mom, and he yelled at us. His body hurt so he turned to alcohol, and he turned towards pain meds and slowly he slipped away again. Eventually, my mom took my little siblings. She left while he was in a stupor one day and started a new life. She started a new family. I never really understood why she didn't take me, but... I was 10 and I was defiant and maybe I was too much like my dad. I choked on the grief of losing my mom and living with a shell of my dad and I continued on in life.

I'd not ever been great at school, so I only went a few hours a day, dropped off and picked up by the "short bus" and glad my friends didn't care. My dad was embarrassed of me though, he told me all the time that I was stupid and slow and that's the only reason my mom had left me. I tried to tell myself he was just messed up inside, but his words stung almost as much as her leaving.

Then one day, the short bus dropped me off outside our little run-down home, I hopped out, walked up to the front door, and found it locked. I couldn't remember a time ever in my life, that this door was locked. I walked around the house and peered through the windows. It looked as if a tornado had struck, but had only targeted the inside of this house, and left me entirely alone.

I went back to the front step and sat down. The moment I leaned against the door frame to wait for my dad, my cat Theo appeared. She was an ethereal little creature, she was silver like a mist rising off the mountains, always moving silently through the world like a little spell. She could tell I was upset and dutifully curled up in my lap.

We waited.

It was late fall in the Columbia gorge and the air was damp and cold. I remembered the ice sliding off the side windows of the school bus as we'd rolled to school that morning. I zipped my sweatshirt up tightly and huddled into it for warmth. When the night finally settled completely over us, the street light clicked on at the nearest corner and I found myself staring at its warm light. I told myself the light was somehow getting into my skin and warming me, and I fell asleep like that.

I woke with a start as the first rays of light drifted over the tops of the steep cliffs that overshadowed this little Washington town. I learned something beautiful and amazing in that moment as the cold shook me awake. During these transition months of spring and autumn, the frost doesn't come until the sunlight does. The sun rose, the temperature dropped, and I watched the frost crawl across my sweatshirt and the windows of my house. I was mesmerized by the climbing white layer which spread across everything I saw and made it sparkle in the sunrise. The beauty of it pushed the cold from my mind completely.

In the distance I heard the brakes of a school bus a couple blocks away. It must be almost time for my bus to show up. My stomach growled. I was going to be so glad for free breakfast today. I saw the bus coming up the road, so I hopped up, brushed the ice from my clothes, put my mask on, and walked down to the corner to start my day. These days they wouldn't let you in school without a mask. It was weird but it was becoming a part of life since Covid last spring. I just wanted to see my friends and have some warm food and forget about everything for awhile.

It went like this for three nights. Theo keeping me warm while I slept outside the house, hoping my dad would come home. I thought about breaking in, sleeping in my own bed, and changing clothes but honestly, I was scared. If my dad didn't want me in there and he came home and found me in there - I don't know what he'd do. I wasn't going to risk it. I kept waiting through the cold nights and started wearing my gym clothes for an extra layer to keep warm.

I believed my dad would come back.

Friday arrived and I asked my buddy Chris if I could stay the night at his place. I stayed there a lot, and his parents liked me. They agreed right away.

I wish I could say I was a good friend to Chris, but I wasn't. I laid there on his carpet under the blankets I'd borrowed, and I thought about my dad and the cold of the three nights I'd slept outside.

What would I do tomorrow? I should have rested but I couldn't stop my brain from churning. I needed to make a plan. Quietly I sat up and listened to the house. Chris's family was sound asleep. I grabbed my school pack, an old camo backpack my dad had given me. I emptied the contents into the floor. There was absolutely nothing useful in there. You can't eat a 5 subject binder. I shoved the contents under Chris's bed. I took my borrowed blanket and rolled it up and tucked it firmly into the pillow case I was using. I walked quickly into the kitchen. I thought of how hungry I'd been for the last few nights, and I shoved several packages of chili and ramen into my pack. I hesitated before I headed for the front door.

On the refrigerator in Chris's kitchen was a whiteboard where they'd all write their requests for the next grocery trip. I grabbed the dry erase marker and quickly scrawled a message: *"I'm sorry, I didn't know what else to do. -Nick."*

I walked out the door and into the night without a plan. I knew I couldn't stay in this town. My home was not here anymore.

I was sure I had to be careful, I was wandering through my small town with a large pack in the middle of the night and if anybody saw me, they'd remember. The stolen cans of chili weighed very heavily in my pack as I moved off the road and into the dark shadows of the forests surrounding town.

Chili was a stupid reason to be a fugitive, but I'd been desperate. I decided to stop by my house one last time, somehow still hopeful that my dad would be back. The place was dark and cold and only Theo appeared to greet me. I felt a tinge of guilt. I'd almost abandoned her like my folks abandoned me. My stomach turned and I dropped to one knee, "Hi Theo, I didn't forget you," I lied as I scuffled her cheek. "Want to go on an adventure with me?" I scooped her up, tucked her in my sweatshirt, and headed into the forest.

I started out with a pretty good idea where I wanted to go, the Pacific Crest Trail cut through these woods. My friends and I had hiked up to it many times over the years. I was going to connect with the trail and head north towards Canada. I was a mountain kid and heading the other direction didn't seem right.

If I'd been an experienced hiker, if I'd have had time to research, if I'd know anything about anything, I'd have known that people don't head north on the PCT in November. Unknowingly I set out with determination, walking until sun rise and then walking all day. Theo and I did take frequent breaks. She meandered and since I didn't really have a destination or schedule, I let her set us on a wanderers pace. Occasionally she'd act tired, and I'd tuck her back into my sweatshirt and let her rest while I kept walking.

It was probably around lunch time that day when we came to a little meadow and then a magnificent waterfall on the other side. I took a risk and stood at the falls and filled my hands and drank until my stomach was full of water. I'd brought a couple bottles of water with me but only been sipping sparingly all day, I wasn't sure how far I'd have to hike before I'd reach another trail town.

There at the waterfall, I didn't hold back, I drank until my sides ached and let the ice water creep into my forehead and give me brain freeze like a 7-11 Slurpee. The air had been frigid all day but since I was hiking, I was really hot. The cold water invigorated me.

I sat there next to the creek and just out of reach of the mist radiating from the base of the falls and let the sun warm my body again. The grass of the meadow called to me and without deciding, I found myself a comfortable spot and fell asleep in afternoon heat. I don't know how long I slept but when I startled awake the sun was close to the horizon.

My mind took a quick inventory and then I noticed something out of place. A strange scratching sound followed by a murmur. The distant babbling blended with the creek nearby and together brought a very old memory. I was young, asleep on a couch in a beam of sunlight, and I could hear my mom and aunties visiting in the kitchen a short distance away. Their voices carried across the house but not loudly enough to make out any real words. You could only hear the emotion... joy... love. It was the last Thanksgiving with my mom. I hadn't know it at the time.

There I was, almost 4 years later, and suddenly the memory brought tears. Where were my aunties? My grandma? Why did nobody come for me? Was I broken in some way that I could never understand? Was I flawed?

I lost all control for a moment as the world around me blurred behind my tears. I felt little Theo push her head into the palm of my hand insistently, trying to comfort me in some way.

I heard the murmur again, only this time it was louder... loud enough that it wasn't the creek or my own thoughts drifting. I rubbed the arm of my shirt across my face, clearing the tears and my vision as I stood up and looked around.

That's when I saw her. The little grey hen, scratching in the dirt along side the river bank, searching for a snack and babbling at the universe.

I walked towards her and bent over to look more closely. She squatted when I did and made it super easy to scoop her up. She was such a strange little creature, definitely a chicken but she was... fluffy? Her feathers were almost like fur, and she had the cutest crown of fluff on her head and was even fluffy on her toes.

"Hello little Hen," I said as I peered at the creature, "what are you doing way out here?" I asked as if she would answer.

"Alone."

The word echoed in my mind, like my inner voice, but not my voice at all. I looked at Hen in shock.

"Yes, alone," I replied, "I'm alone out here too... well kinda, I have Theo here," and I nodded towards the cat.

"Alone," the voice echoed again.

"Sorry about that, I don't know how on Earth you'd possibly end up out here alone," I said, acknowledging her word.

"Old," she said and seemed to nuzzle into my arm.

"You're alone because you're old?" I asked her. My answer was a sad blink and a long stretch of silence.

"I'm sorry somebody abandoned you. I was... "the words hesitated as I tried to form them, "I was abandoned also."

There in the layers afternoon sunlight, our eyes made contact, and so did our spirits. I made up my mind, "Well, I don't care if you're old, little Hen, I'll keep you safe." I promised her, and I intended to keep that promise.

It was officially getting late in the day. A glance at the horizon reminded me that the sunset would come suddenly and would not have mercy for my schedule.

I made a decision to stay in the meadow by the creek for the night. I'd spend the last of the daylight making us a camp and settle in rather than traveling farther up the trail.

I busied myself setting out my bedroll, prying open a can of chili and feeding myself and my two little companions.

"Thanks for the food, Chris," I said to the empty meadow as my stomach finally stopped aching and the food settled in.

I climbed into my blankets, with little Hen and Theo both snuggled in as well, and quickly sleep overcame me. The afternoon nap hadn't held the exhaustion of those lonely nights away for long.

I dreamed of fire. I saw a group of strangers, choking for air under a storm cloud made entirely of smoke. I saw the fear in their eyes as they ran from the flames that consumed entire landscapes. I did not know that somewhere far south, on this same trail, a small group of humans had just hatched the ancient Phoenix. Hundreds of miles from where I'd slept, Phoenix had risen in a magical inferno which touched off the largest real wildfire in recorded history. Somehow, in my dreams, I was a witness. I saw the children as they wove the very magic which woke the sleeping goddess. I saw the fear when they realized their mistake, and I saw the grief when instead of saving them, the goddess abandoned them to the flames.

There in that meadow, for myself and my two companions, a different storm was building. If I'd have been awake, I'd have felt the forest go silent as the moonlight went dark, smothered behind storm clouds that gathered on the mountain tops around us. I'd have felt the first cold breeze as it carried a fine cold rain across our little camp and then froze the air around us. I'd have felt the cold, cold rain seep into my bedding and turn to ice. Instead, I slept on as the icy rain turned into snow and began to blanket everything around me.

Instead of my own peril, I was lost in the trauma of the children as they plunged into a river and drifted towards the ocean, a last attempt to escape the fires which would kill many that night.

"Help!!!!" the word penetrated my sleeping mind and suddenly I was awake. I sat up out of the snow and felt the ice cracking on my pants. They were stiff and so cold. I felt for Theo and Hen and found them soaked to the skin, with their fur frozen and brittle.

We were freezing to death.

The thought hit me suddenly and I stood up, clumping the ice and snow off of my body. I had no matches, no lighter, no way to warm us up. My mind felt muddled, the dream still clung so strongly that I could smell the smoke. My feet felt like they were two bricks as I tried to stomp myself free of the cold. Under my head, my dad's old military pack was still dry inside.

I huddled ridiculously in the bag, which barely covered my head and shoulders, while I began to brush the ice off of Theo and Hen. Theo didn't even respond and for a moment I thought she was already dead. A tear sprung to my eye and the lashes clung together, freezing immediately.

"How the hell did this happen?" I mumbled aloud, watching my words freeze in the air around me, "It was a beautiful day yesterday."

I'd lived there my entire life and I knew a Pacific northwest storm could hit hard and fast... but I'd never once seen it like this. It was as if the very flame that heated me from within had left the earth while I slept, only leaving cold in its wake.

I thought of my dream, of the children's grief as they realized that Phoenix had abandoned them. I huddled under the pack and the cold seemed to seep deeper. Little Hen murmured and shivered in my lap, her hair tuft frozen in an absurd clump on one side of her tiny head.

We were freezing to death.

I looked at Hen and Theo and it slowly dawned on me. My dads pack could never shelter me from a storm like this, but it might just save these two little spirits. I scooped them up and walked towards the trees bordering the meadow. Under their canopy the snow was less pressing, they sheltered us all. I stumbled into the forest a little ways, the creeping numbness making my body feel strongly detached and uncooperative.

I found an old brick wall, clinging to the foundation of a house that was only a memory. The smooth side comforted me, so I huddled next to the wall and carefully emptied my pack of all its belongings. I set it on its side like a little cave, and then I tucked Theo and Hen inside. I set the pack in my lap to put some space between the two little ones and the frozen ground below and I hugged the pack close to my body and breathed warm air into the pocket where they slept. Occasionally I reached inside to check on them. Miraculously they were warm and dry. I leaned against the wall, and I glanced at the canopy above, a dancing wall of shadows kept me from seeing the stars above, and from seeing the massive bird, sitting there in the night watching me.

Phoenix.

I let the cold settle in, and I let my body become the shelter that I hoped might save my two little friends. Slowly an unnatural sense of warmth spread over my body and my thoughts started to dim. I'd read somewhere long ago that freezing to death was a lot like going to sleep, and in the last moments, it would even feel warm.

I let the deceitful warm comfort me, and as I drifted off my mind went to my parents. Why had they abandoned me? I thought of Phoenix. Why was she abandoning us? Then the fog consumed me, and I let go of my body.

Once I was asleep, the fog turned into thick and dangerous smoke. While my body froze to death, my mind was trapped in an inferno. There, at the center of the flames, was the creator. Phoenix.

"Why am I here?" I begged her for answers.

"I'm not sure, Son, I came here for Hen," she replied, her words crackling like a log splitting in a fire, "I wonder why you meddle in my revenge?"

"Revenge?" I blinked as the smoke stung my eyes and my words came out as a rattling cough, "Why would you ever want revenge against Hen? She's so sweet and simple."

"Lies," she scoffed, "Hen will say she loves you while she shoves you off a cliff and smothers your flames in an entire ocean of rage!" Phoenix screamed and around us the flames leapt up.

"Why would she?" I mumbled, confused as my mind tried to picture little Hen daring to take on the Phoenix. Little Hen, the murderess. It couldn't be true.

"Phoenix, don't lie to the boy, tell him the truth," Hen spoke up as she seemed to manifest from the very smoke itself, "tell him why I drowned you that day."

My eyebrows singed as rage seemed to consume the Phoenix, "If you truly thought I was mad, Hen, why wouldn't you help me instead of hurting me? Why did you pretend to love me?"

"I did love you, Phoenix. You're the other part of the very spark that gives my life meaning. You're everything to me. I've been tormented ever since that day. I never wanted to lose you. I was afraid of your anger. I was afraid you'd destroy humanity... your own children. I had to do something. I regret it every day." Hen replied, the tremble in her voice told us all that every word was true.

"I loved you, too, Hen. I loved you more than myself or my human children. I decided if you wanted me dead, then I must deserve death. I still feel that way. That's why I'm going to leave." Phoenix replied.

"Leave?" Hen repeated, the confusion in her voice clearly hanging on the word.

"Hen," Phoenix replied sadly, "You were right, I'm deeply flawed, and I don't know why. I can't stop hurting you and I can't stop hurting the humans, the very creatures I created to love and nurture. I wish I could stop but instead the jealousy rages and even worse, I see that jealousy in the human spirit, in the very flame that I gifted them with. I thought I'd chosen a special creature and turned them into my family but what I really did was ruin them. The only way to fix what I've done is to take the very spark which dooms them... and leave."

Hen and I looked at Phoenix as a stunned silence stretched between us.

Hen spoke next, "Phoenix, I'm begging you not to leave me again. I can't go on like this. I love you, without you the light goes out of everything."

"I'm sorry, Hen. I love you, too. I thought I came here for revenge, but this boy has shown me that even a broken soul can share love. Even a broken soul can be a protector. I can be brave. I can step away so that my dear children, my humans, might somehow survive and break the awful cycle that I've created."

I found myself humbled as I saw the love and acceptance shared between Hen and Phoenix. I was in the presence of truly powerful and wise beings. Then, as I stood there bearing witness, the two of them embraced.

Steam rose as the water in hens spirit connected with the fire in Phoenix.

"Take me with you," Hen begged as the flames sparked and sizzled.

"I would give anything to take you, Hen, but I can't. I need you to stay here with the humans. They're going to need you," ashes fell from Phoenix' eyes where tears would normally be, and then she rose into the air like a fireball and vanished into the smoke above.

I woke in the forest leaning against the wall. Snow blanketed everything in sight, but around my huddled body, green grass glistened, and steam rose. I was alive, and warm. Something solid and cold rested in my hand, opened my fingers and discovered a small crystal in my palm. It looked like it had swirls of smoke inside but when I tilted it, they vanished, and the stone was oozing glass clear.

There was a rustle from the backpack still tucked in my lap, and two little heads emerged cautiously, Theo and Hen.

I smiled down at them, "Glad we made it, I think the three of us have got some work to do."

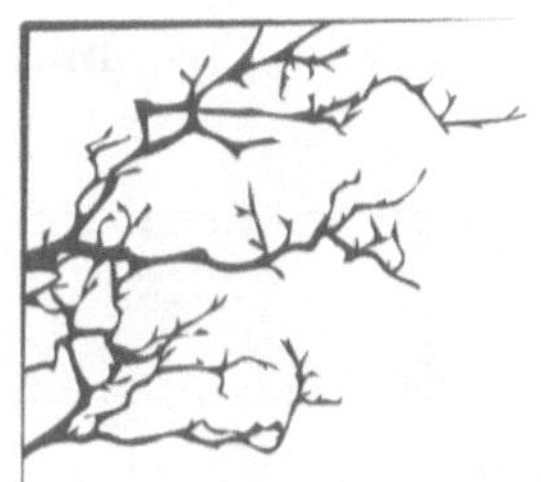

Humm

Aida the disappointment. That was her, the girl who just couldn't stop being weird. The girl who just couldn't get along.

"Aida, look at me."

"Aida, use a calm body."

"Aida stop distracting the class."

"Aida, it's not time to make bird noises! Aida sit still! Aida put your feet on the floor! Aida. Stop. FLAPPING!"

It was like that for me starting on day one. I found myself in kindergarten and when everyone else recited the days of the week my mind drifted to the birds. I mumbled and thought of my new favorite back yard friends and then when everyone else was sitting down for rug time I'd stand up in a burst of energy and spin and leap across the room. "I'm a humming bird!" I'd declare.

"Aida, no, it's not time to spin, Aida! Aida... look at me Aida, come and sit crisscross-applesauce and listen to a story. I'll give you a treat if you can have a calm body for story time."

I always wanted the treat so badly, but my body and my mind simply could NOT *be* calm. The teacher would read away and inside me the birdsong would swell until finally I'd sing, sometimes a tiny peep just above a whisper and sometimes the glorious honk of a goose. I couldn't stop myself.

I think it was around 4th grade that things went bad for me. The gentle prompts and the rewards vanished, and the angry disappointed faces filled my days. I had all the specialists. My parents met me with angry lectures every night. It would have bothered me, but my mind was in the clouds, soaring with the birds.

I was given a tablet and I was supposed to use it to practice math, my worst subject. Instead, I researched the birds. Every free indoor moment I combed through Wikipedia and Google pages hunting down every drop of information I could. Every free outdoor moment, I spent watching the birds. I know other people call themselves "bird watchers" but I wasn't just watching. I was a bird person, and I was sure the birds knew it as well.

Years went by, and my obsession and my knowledge just kept growing. Much to my teachers dismay, I'd not ever found any way to control my urges and the closest I ever came to following their curriculum was when I could make the topic turn towards the birds. I did great in biology but when I was supposed to be writing about the coral reefs, I wrote about sea birds. In art class I sketched, painted, sculpted and constructed birds of all sorts. They were sometimes scientifically accurate and sometimes fantastical winged creatures from my mind.

There were teachers that really worked with me and my bird brain but there were others who somehow seemed to take it personally. I wasn't defying them. I could only do what my heart would let me, and my heart was with the birds. I did the best I could every day, and for some teachers it just wasn't good enough.

They started identifying me for "services" and before I knew it, I was spending less and less time with my friends and more and more time with "professionals." Occupational therapy, social skills, communication coaching, and so ...many ...doctors. It seemed like every single adult in my life wanted me to be a different person and none of them wanted me to be me.

I really tried, but instead of thinking about the birds less, I thought of them more. In fact, I'd begun to have a sneaking suspicion. I'd learned dozens of bird songs and started singing them back at the birds and over time, well, we'd started talking. Not just mimicking each other but I mean, really communicating. If anything, my conversations with the birds were easier than with the humans around me.

Was it all in my head? I didn't know.

What I did know was that I lived in a world that was right next to my peers but entirely different from theirs. I was truly an imposter among humans. I got quieter and quieter at school, it was an effort to get people to stop LOOKING at me. I hated the stares, and it was obvious that nobody seemed to like what they saw.

I'd spend the hours trying to vanish into my chair, staring out the window hoping to see any feathered friend flutter by. I'd learned to mostly tune out the class lecture, nearly leaving my body behind and drifting somewhere in the skies above. I loved history class. Don't get me wrong I hate the subject, but history class was positioned parallel to a little courtyard and one of the planters out there had a flowering shrub that the hummingbirds adored. I watched them dance the hour away and the class was survivable.

I had two classes with no windows, PE and tech lab. I wish I could tell you how I despised them. The minutes would stretch out until it seemed I was in my own kind of purgatory. I stared at the clock, and I willed it to jump forward to the end of the hour so that I might at least find a desk by a window for my next period.

It went on like that for months, maybe years, since every minute somehow seemed to stretch eternal. Whatever else was happening I stared at the clock, willing it to set me free. I never did PE with the class, if I asked the teacher would let me run laps alone. I trotted and I stared at the clock, and I begged it to skip forward and free me from that day's torment.

And then, one day... it did.

I was rounding the corner to complete lap 5 billion and glaring angrily at the clock which demanded I spend 13 more minutes in hell and suddenly I heard a humming. It wasn't a normal sound, it was like the rapid fluttering of hummingbird wings echoed in my head. My steps faltered, and then the world skipped.

My classmates were no longer involved in a gripping game of kickball and were already trailing into the locker room to get ready for the next class. The PE teacher was staring at me with an odd look on his face.

"Aida, what are you doing? I told everyone to wrap it up! You're going to be late for your next class," he demanded and tweeted his whistle at me, as if it would remind me how to walk again.

I looked up at the clock, my old nemesis and discovered 13 minutes had vanished in the flutter of a bird wing.

I started towards the locker room, my mind reeling. What the hell just happened?

The rest of the day felt floaty and weird. It was like I was standing just behind my own self, watching me finish my last class and then floating home instead of walking. I felt totally out of my body. I hovered through the evening and fell asleep without really ever having another clear thought, because the one thought was pressing everything else out of my mind: did I just skip-hop through time?!?

The next day was different, I woke up clear headed and with a poignant memory of the skip I'd done the day before. It had happened and it had happened because that's what I wanted. I made it happen. I wondered if I could make it happen again.

I could. I spent the next few weeks teaching myself to humm on demand and skip forward in 13 minute increments. I had no idea why 13 was my lucky number but I learned to love it. Never again would I sit through a boring tech class lecture. In fact, I basically time-skipped through every class but history, where I'd pause, rest, and visit the hummingbirds at the window.

There I was, sitting in that desk, the closest desk to those windows where I always sat during history when I saw something I'd never expected. A humming bird flittered by and looked directly at me...

followed by another, and then finally a third hummingbird hovered there. They held my eyes and then, while I watched, they did a sky dance, and vanished.

"What?!?" I said aloud, and then with a rapid humming sound everything seemed to rewind. I wasn't sure how far back I went, maybe about a minute, but there I was still sitting and staring out that window when the first bird appeared for a second time... then another, and finally a third. Moments later, they danced, and then disappeared.

"What the hell!" I blurted out and found myself suddenly standing at the window and out of my desk.

"Aida, take a seat. Aida, we're talking about the history of the railroad, Aida. Do you have anything to add?" The teacher glared at me as I interrupted her annoyed questions.

"Did anybody else SEE THAT?!?" I asked again.

"Aida! You're distracting the class."

I cut her off, surely somebody else had been looking out the window... there was thirty people crammed in this room, "Did anybody see what those hummingbirds did?!?"

"Okay, Aida, that's enough, this is history class. I need you to go take a break at the vice principals office." The teacher was absolutely fed up with me. I knew it bugged her that I never made eye contact, never did homework, never participated. That's not why I came to history class. I was here for the humming birds.

I got up out of my seat and scowled at the teacher, "Honestly I'm not going to waste my time in here listening to you talk about the railroads like they weren't built on the sacrifices of Chinese workers who were left to die from exposure when they'd finished making a profit for the rail companies. I have no reason to waste my time in a history class like this." I walked out proudly, and instead of going to the office I took a quick left and headed towards the court yard and the humming bird bush.

I was at the side doors about to pop one open with my hip and rip my mask off, when I saw him. He was a kid I vaguely recognized from the special classes and the waiting rooms of the therapists and the short bus. He was hunched over in a funny way with his bag held in front of him and cradled like a puppy. I looked at him.

For a moment, we made eye contact.

Then I saw it. Grief. Not the quiet weeping grief you might expect, but a grief that clung to his entire spirit in the form of rage. This time my mind really processed what I was seeing. He was partway through the process of taking a gun out of his bag.

A gun.

A gun in school.

We looked at each other. We both looked up the hallway, and as we did, another student walked around the corner. He saw us and started yelling. The fire alarm suddenly went off. My mind raced and, in that moment, I knew I had to do something.

It couldn't be like this. Not now, not here... not anywhere. I let the humming in my mind unleash and rapidly time slipped backwards.

I was standing at the door again and this time he still had his backpack on his shoulders.

"Hey," I said, calling to him. He looked up at me, his eyes filled with the same grief I'd seen moments before, "hey isn't your name Ian?"

"Yeah," he mumbled, not really looking at me, his eyes glancing around nervously.

"Can you help me with something?" I asked. Anything to distract him from the path I knew he was walking.

"Help you?" he repeated at me, this time his eyes fluttering from their distant focus and onto mine. We made eye contact.

"Yeah, I just saw something crazy, and Mrs. K is an ass. She kicked me out of class..." I didn't know what I was doing but I finally just said the truth, "I swear I just saw some humming birds vanish." I declared.

He looked at me, this time with recognition in his eyes, "OH," he kind of laughed, "you're the BIRD brain girl." He smiled at me.

I winced a little, I hated the nickname given by classmates to single me out as a wierdo. "Yeah, that's me, the bird brain" I answered, and then suddenly I remembered exactly WHO Ian was.

I remembered when they'd taken his backpack and strewn it all over the playground. They'd ripped his artwork up and called him a r*%@*d.

I remembered when classmates caught him walking home alone in January and threw him in an ice capped creek. He'd almost drowned that day and suffered a nearly deadly case of hypothermia.

I remembered the time his mom had shown up drunk to school, found him on the playground and slapped him right in front of everyone. She was furious he'd forgotten to take the trash out before school. She stumbled away while he held his face, and everyone laughed.

I remembered the names and the taunts and suddenly I remembered how much Ian was like me.

I repeated myself, "Yeah so... yeah, I'm the Bird Brain Girl and I remember you. Will you help me?"

He hesitated, subconsciously adjusting his backpack straps. I wondered how heavy it was, not just the gun but his intentions. So. Very. Heavy. He looked at me closely like he needed to see the truth in my eyes and when he did, he nodded a little, "Okay, I'll help you."

The two of us pushed the side door open and headed out into the courtyard, behind us a student rounded a corner in the hallway, just in time to see the door snap shut again.

I pushed the contents of his pack out of my mind and walked towards the hummingbird bush, "they were right here and then it was like they were dancing in the air, and they simply vanished."

He looked at me a little doubtfully and smirked, "Do you see vanishing birds, often?" He asked.

"No," I answered, "In fact I stare at them for hours every day and I never saw anything like this, and actually, it happened twice."

He seemed to think about my words and then suddenly he took his backpack off, dropped it to the ground next to him and squatted next to the bush, looking up into its branches from below, "I bet there's a tiny nest in here," he suggested.

I thought about grabbing the pack and instead I plopped down next to him and peered at the branches. There was no sign of the birds, just the jutting of branches into the blue sky above. Something small and round pressed into my leg, I felt around and picked up a small dark agate with milk white clouds swirling along its surface. I tucked the agate in my pocket and looked up at the bush.

Then, as we laid there, the birds appeared, hovering only inches from our faces. I could feel the wing beats humming above us, and it almost seemed as if they sucked the entire oxygen out of the air around us. I gasped as Ian and I sat up. We were now face to face with 3 humming birds, watching as they danced. This time they didn't vanish like before, they held our eyes for several heartbeats and then they darted off towards the hillside behind the football field.

The hillside.

We both froze as our eyes processed what we were seeing.

The hillside. Engulfed in flames.

"Holy shit!" I uttered in shock, "Ian... call 911!"

We both scrambled for our phones and anxiously pressed the home buttons.

Nothing.

"What's going on? My battery is dead?" Ian said, an edge of panic in his voice. I realized my phone was also dead.

"I don't know!" I replied in a rush, "We have to warn people! We have to get everyone out of here!" I realized we only had moments to spare, as a thick wall of smoke suddenly darkened the sky above.

We ran for the door we'd just come out of and discovered it was stuck. Electric locks, designed to keep a stranger from walking in and shooting up our school, now engaged and refusing to budge. I thought about Ian's backpack. The doors were stuck shut, frozen in the locked position when the electricity failed.

My mind blamed the fire. As a kid growing up in Northern California wildfire country, you never stop thinking about the fire. My Uncle died in the Camp fire in Paradise only a couple years ago and as Ian and I took turns yanking on that frozen door I thought of him. There was no rescue call because the lines were dead, there was no chance to escape. I glanced towards the hillside, and I thought of Uncle Ernie, and I realized that if we didn't do something soon, we'd all die that day.

"Ian let's try the gym doors, they're old with the locking bars," I suggested as we ran through a courtyard and around the side of the building towards the front of the school. It was so crazy, as soon as we were around the corner of the building the day seemed perfect. There was no sign of the incoming wall of fire. We'd all known that about a hundred miles away the Bear fire was burning but nobody inside had ANY idea that the Bear had turned towards us.

Nobody, that is, except me and Ian.

The gym ran along the side of the building where recent renovations had stopped. The gym, the shop, the stage and the art room were all still built like they'd been back in the 60s or 70s.

No fancy electric locks on this older wing of the school, but of course the giant old doors were manually locked. Ian and I could hear the sound of bouncing basketballs reverberating from inside, the 10th grade PE class was in there this period. We tried pounding but between the thick old doors, the shouting of teens and the steady thumping of the ball, nobody heard us.

We paused and looked at each other, "use it," I said, nodding towards his backpack.

"Use it?" He shook his head, confused as he stepped back.

"Use the gun, shoot this lock, get this damn door open before we have to listen to people burn to death in there!!!" I said in a rushed response.

He looked at me grimly, but he didn't make any half hearted denials. He slipped his backpack off, unzipped the computer pocket and pulled a hand gun out of it. I think my heart actually stopped for a moment and his eyes met mine. I could see the pain and guilt.

"Don't think about it," I said and touched his arm reassuringly, "Just do the right thing, right now."

He nodded and we both took a few steps back and he pointed the gun at the giant old keyhole lock on the doors.

"Do you know how to use it?" I asked him.

"Yeah." He answered.

"Is it safe to stand here?" I followed up.

"I think so, I'm not positive. Plug your ears." He waited for me to shove my fingers in my ears then took a deep breath and pulled the trigger. Part of the door panel came off. He cocked the gun, pointed it at the second door and pulled the trigger again.

Nothing happened.

He looked at his gun, confused, then did several little things with it before trying to fire it again.

"I don't know what's wrong, I guess it's broken," he said, looking at me. I watched as he opened the place with the bullets, emptied them one by one, and tossed them in a nearby garbage can. He put the empty and apparently broken gun in his backpack. "I should probably just throw it away, but it feels wrong to leave it in the school garbage." He said to me, matter-of-factly.

I nodded in agreement and then both of us started yanking on the door with the broken lock. Thankfully, it was broken enough to open, and we ran inside, frantic to warn as many people as we could. The class inside had ended, and the students were in the locker rooms, Ian and I ran in and started shouting:

"Fire! Clear the building! Fire!"

I don't know if I've ever shouted so loudly and for so long. Together we raced the hallways of the school, screaming at the top of our lungs:

"Fire! Get out through the gym! Fire!"

Word spread quickly and suddenly the halls surged with students and teachers. We were a small school but when every SINGLE body was in the hallway and on the same evacuation route, the place seemed very crowded.

It was probably less than 10 minutes later, and the entire school was evacuated to the parking lot on the front side of the building. This was the farthest side from the fire. The parking lot was huge, making room for buses, student and staff vehicles and having a huge drop off zone and then a row of outdoor basketball and tennis courts. This school had been designed with defensible space. These were intentionally cleared and paved areas, to protect us from the constant threat of wildfire. They started changing the way schools in fire country are built after multiple towns burned to the ground and dozens died. This school was meant to be safe.

We reached the parking lot and quickly teachers organized by homeroom and took a role call. Everyone was safely outside the building. The buses weren't there, and since it was the middle of the day, they were not due for hours. Quickly the principal and VP made a plan, and everyone started loading into every personal vehicle in the parking lot.

Not every student drove and there wouldn't be nearly enough seats, so people piled in like it was a clown car challenge, 8 people crammed into a 17 year old's hatchback. All over the parking lot, people squished into vehicles preparing to get out of the path of the fire.

None of the cars would start.

Panic spread through the crowd.

We had no way of knowing that just a few miles from here, the Phoenix had risen, leaving behind a wake of flames. Then in an act of desperation, she'd vanished, taking all of our power with her.

There would be no more cars, no more cell phones, no more guns. These things, this spark of power which humanity attributed to science and to fossil fuels and to electricity - these things had never ONCE belonged to humans. They'd been a gift from Phoenix, and she'd taken them back.

There we were, and nothing worked. The only flame was the heat of the Phoenix-born wildfires bearing down on us. I watched as the panic spread faster than the flames. I looked over at Ian and I knew he had the same realization as me. We'd gotten everyone out of the building, but we still might die out here.

I thought of my uncle, dead in his own driveway. Was I about to die in this driveway two years later??? I thought of the birds. Why would they warn me but not in time to save me? I glanced towards the sky and the trees on the far side of the parking lot.

That's when I saw them, the three hummingbirds, hovering there as though they'd been waiting, patiently, for me to notice them. I nudged Ian with my elbow and pointed. Without saying a word, we both walked towards them.

I doubt any of us really thought about it anymore, the ancient mine which had once existed here at the same place as our new school. The company had built a kind of canal which ran from the dig, past this location and into the lake about a mile from here. Miraculously, this unnatural canal was actually holding water. It was a vibrant pulsing stream about knee deep, winding its way out of the fire which was rapidly descending upon us all.

We started shouting for attention and before long everyone in the parking lot moved towards the unnatural spring. The water felt so welcoming as it ran around my ankles, pulling us towards safety. I looked at Ian and realized he wasn't in the little channel yet.

"Let's go," I nodded down stream and gestured towards the other evacuees.

"I'm going to make sure everyone is out of the parking lot before I go, Aida." He smiled at me and said with resolve.

"Then I'll stay too," I replied, and started to step back out of the water.

"No, you get safe, I'll be right behind you," he reassured me.

I hesitated but something in Ian's eyes told me he needed to stay until he was sure he'd saved every life out there that day. I understood with out him saying. I stepped up next to him and wrapped in in a giant hug that nearly knocked us both over. I looked closely into his eyes, "I KNOW you're a hero, Ian, and I'll see you on the flip side."

I jumped back down into the water and started wading towards safety. Around me, other teens and teachers also trudged along towards the lake, a march to safety and away from the flames leaping at our backs.

I did not see the condor soaring over head nor the little companion following below. I had no way of knowing that the Death Doulas were there for my new friend.

Ian, once I was out of sight, had set himself upon a mission. He hurriedly returned to the hummingbird bush in the little courtyard and quickly he'd ducked below the branches again as glowing ashes rained down from the sky.

There it was, the hummingbird nest he'd spotted nearly a lifetime ago, in the moments before he and Aida had seen the fire. The tiny nest cradled between several branches was still there, waiting for his rescue. Deftly he broke the branches away from the bush, being careful not to jostle the hummingbird eggs. He trotted back towards the gym and quickly went into the supply closet. There he found a bag of red rubber balls and dragged it towards the old canal. He strode down into the canal, secured the branches to the ball bag, and shoved the entire makeshift raft downstream.

He hoped the little life raft would make it safely to the lake and somehow the birds would be saved. He thought of Moses and the hope he'd brought. His own heart swelled with hope.

The school behind him ignited and hot ashes began to scorch his hair and skin. Within moments the world around him was an inferno. Ian didn't feel the heat. He'd already succumbed to the smoke. His mind was somewhere in the skies far, far above, soaring with the condor.

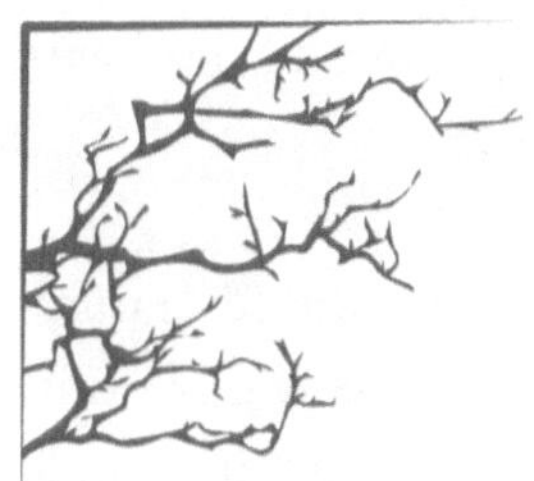

Crescendo

Niyi ran as soon as he could walk. He was proud of his swift feet, but it was his mind that his mother noticed. Niyi mastered everything presented to him with little effort, racing through his lessons and then racing to run through the fields after.

He simply wanted to run.

His elders encouraged the running and told him: "Sprint through the fields, chase away the Quelea, you can be the protector of our crops. You'll be a young hero!"

This is why Niyi woke before the sun and raced through his studies so that he may race through the fields and save his people. He knew he had an important destiny, and he ran towards it joyfully and with pride.

He was seven when the first true Quelea storm arrived.

Niyi paused in his running to watch a butterfly flitter about when a chubby little red-headed bird landed in front of him. He knew right away what it was, defending against Quelea was his main occupation.

There was never just one.

Niyi looked up as the sky darkened, a flock so thick that it seemed it would keep coming forever. He shouted and grabbed the branches he used to make himself bigger and began racing the fields. He sang at the top of his lungs as he swatted and rushed and jumped and danced and did all he could to make the fields too hostile for the bird raiders. They chose his neighbor's field, standing vulnerable and unprotected by a young runner, and like a plague they descended upon it.

Within moments it was as if the field were alive, swarms of Quelea landing and departing and the earth torn asunder as they clawed through, removing every single seed grain they discovered. Niyi watched on in stunned horror, his arms still flailing above his head with the branches intended to help intimidate and protect.

It was Niyi who felt intimidated.

He looked back towards home, somebody should warn his parents and the neighbors - somebody had to do something. He was the only body there and if he were to try and get to his father, the birds could take their fields as well. He continued dancing as his mind raced.

Like any storm, the entire chaos surged, and with a final frenzy, it was over. The Quelea took to the air in a cacophony and then vanished over the horizon.

Niyi looked upon the devastated fields of his neighbor. It was as though a bomb had gone off. It would be a hungry year for everyone depending on these crops. It was because of this experience that Niyi became obsessed with the Quelea.

"How do other people fight the birds, Father?" he asked.

"With fire and bombs, Son," he answered.

"Fire? And bombs?" Niyi's voice trailed off. His young mind picturing the storm of birds, landing as a massive cloud in the neighbors fields, on fire.

"How do you light a bird on fire? That sounds awful," he asked.

"Oh, not the birds, Son, we go after their nesting grounds."

Niyi was distressed.

His father looked at him kindly, "I know it sounds awful, but it's the most efficient way of making them stop. We need the crops to survive.

"And anyhow Niyi, we do not bomb our feathered enemies in this family. Instead, we have you, our little runner with swift feet and mind. We have no need for bombs, and we can't afford them anyway."

It was on that day that Niyi truly understood his responsibility. He did not only protect the human crops, if he did his job right, he protected the nesting grounds of the Quelea as well. It was because of this responsibility that he became a storm chaser of a different sort. He chased the bird storms across every field he could reach. He ran and ran from sunup until sundown, and he did not stop at the borders of his family fields any longer.

Niyi ran and danced wherever the bird storms flew.

To the adults it seemed as though he ran through the clouds of birds like a child would run through the waves of the ocean, an intricate dance of give and take. The background music was always the thunderous white noise of the Quelea moving: a thousand wingbeats, an ocean of spirits washing across the skyline and onto the fields. Niyi ran, and the wings thundered, and the birds flew and together they danced a survival dance.

No firebombs for Niyi's birds, ever. No more hungry seasons for Niyi's family, ever.

When change came to Niyi's town it was very much like the Quelea storms. Sudden. Deadly. It was not birds, it was a corporation.

They rolled through with a contract. The government gave them special rights to all that was Niyi's world. His neighbors were slowly replaced by one giant unknown entity. Field hands replaced by one machine. Local crops replaced by one mega crop. Local ways of living replaced rapidly by singular ideas and innovation.

Then one morning, at age ten, Niyi finished his book work and raced to the fields like always. There, he discovered no place for a field runner.

A giant steel faced man grabbed him by his arm.

"Where are you going?" he demanded.

"To run with the Quelea," responded young Niyi.

"Go back and ask your parents for a different chore, we have a new plan for the Quelea," responded the angry stranger.

"I have to run with the Quelea to keep them off the crops," repeated Niyi, his feet and mind yearning for the race, excited for the day's dance.

"Oh, we'll keep those red-headed devils off these crops, we've sent a team to the nesting grounds," he patted Niyi dismissively and pushed him towards home.

"A team to the nesting grounds?!?" Niyi stepped back, shaking his head, thinking of his sky family, thinking of the miles he'd run to protect everyone, thinking of the dances.

"What will you do?" He asked, tears springing to his eyes. His life's work threatened as the sun continued to rise.

"They're going to the closest nesting grounds and light them up. The only way to kill these things is with fire before they ever take flight," the man glanced upwards towards the skies, often darkened with Quelea, and when he looked back down Niyi had vanished.

He was running.

He visited the nesting grounds often. He'd kept them a secret, in his hopes to protect the Quelea, but of course the corporate men had found them anyways. When they hunted, they didn't stop until everyone suffered, he thought, as he ran on towards his feathered friends. Alongside him a storm began to gather. A thunderous cloud of Quelea paced him and darted about in a frenzy.

The thunder of their wings was no longer a chaotic cacophony of white noise, but instead, from within the wild sound, Niyi began to hear words.

"Help! Help us! Save our young! Help us!" The Quelea shouted as he ran.

Tears streaked Niyi's face and heat burned through his lungs as his desperation propelled him past exhaustion and forward on his mission.

He had to stop those bombs.

"Help us, please Niyi, please help us!" The thunderous demands deafening him as he rushed forward, blinded by panic.

The working men were also blinded, by the flames of their own ambition. Oblivious to the horror they unfurled.

They did not see Niyi as he approached, running faster than he'd ever run. They had no time to stop, even had they tried. Niyi, without a thought for himself, rushed headlong into the flames.

Anything to protect his Quelea.

The flames were rapidly doused by workers who screamed in horror as they saw a small child jump into the fire. People rushed to find little Niyi in the ashes. Around them, frantic Quelea also searched for their nests and their dead. This child had been willing to die for them, for a bird which tormented the human crops and was seen as vermin. This boy was special.

The child was found sprawled amongst the nests and still cradling several eggs in his shirt. The shirt now scorched and strewn with ashes.

Carefully the humans loaded him onto one of the giant machines and started towards his home. Every soul watched as Niyi, his body covered in blisters and his mind lost in the flames, struggled for each breath.

The Quelea queen was among them, fluttering about in a cloud surrounded by her flock and watching as the humans rushed to save Niyi. She'd watched many seasons, and secretly, she loved him.

The humans below had arrived at Niyi's family home, and they all shouted.

"You've killed our SON!" his mother screamed and flung herself on the workmen, enraged.

"Please, he ran in so quickly. Nobody could stop him! Why was he out here?!" A giant formidable man demanded as he pulled the distraught woman from his body and held her away from him.

"This is his JOB! He always does the running! You are the ones who shouldn't be here!"

Niyi's father spoke up, "He does this for all of us! He does this because he is kind, and he is hard working. How dare you imply he was doing the wrong thing? He did what he knew to do, he ran, and he protected us!"

The argument strengthened as little Niyi weakened. The adults shouting as though his spirit were already gone. The Queen looked on as the spark in Niyi began to dim.

It was then that she made the decision. She would save Niyi.

She began to sing. She sang the song of a hero, a dancer, a child. She sang the song of Niyi. Within her words she wove the spark of life which propelled all humans, the spark of the Phoenix. This is not all she wove into little Niyi. The child, who seemed to generate endless energy from his very soul, was about to run out, so she gave him hers. In the music she wove the power of a thousand wing beats, the massive energy of a Quelea storm at its peak, moving as one. A force of nature. She put those wing beats into Niyi: a thousand wings thumping with every heartbeat.

The spell took hold and there on the little stretcher, Niyi found his spark again. He reached out to his parents.

"Papa, I'm here Papa."

The sound of Niyi's voice stopped everything. Nobody standing there could deny that where a dying child had just been, now there was a bright eyed miracle.

The Queen, satisfied with her decision, left them. She returned to the nesting grounds. She had her own dead to mourn.

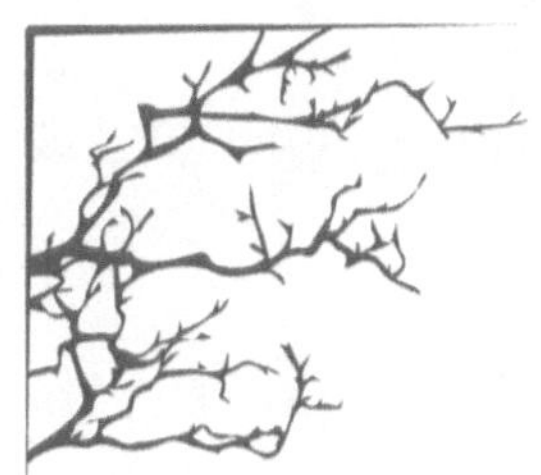

Hatch

It's weird growing up without a mom, but you get used to it. My dad reminded me often, "a boy needs his dad." It sounds encouraging, I know, but it comes with the unspoken "and it doesn't matter that your mom left."

The thing is, it does matter to me, I think about it every single day. And lately I don't even feel much like a boy. It's hard to explain, but I know I can't talk to my dad about it, somehow, in some way, me being his son makes a lot of other things easier for him to cope with. The heartbreak and the grief are shoved deep below the surface and masked with pride. My dad is the proudest. He never misses a game, he never misses a conference, he somehow figures out what I'm into every year and he gives the best Christmas gifts. I know he loves me, but it hurts badly to face the reality: my dad hardly knows me at all.

Everyday the burden builds, I feel as if I'm carrying this lie and I also feel as if I can never talk to my dad without hurting him. Why does my identity even affect him? I'll never understand.

The easiest way to keep a secret is to just stay busy, and I lived my life like that. I buried myself in Polynesian culture, I knew my mom was Polynesian so I read anything and everything I could get my hands on. I used google like other folks used a family bible, delving into the past and into a world I belonged too but couldn't be a part of. I was an outsider in every way, a stranger to my culture, my family, and even my own body.

I'd been on a deep dive, researching the flora and fauna of the pacific island cultures when I stumbled on a YouTube channel that changed my life: a channel about raising Emu. I was mesmerized. I wish I could explain the feeling of excitement that crept up my spine, and even more so -the feeling like I'm finally breathing. Like I'd been holding my breath for a lifetime.

Emu.

I watched as a large, nearly dinosaur-like bird turned towards the camera and seemed to nod directly at me. I knew I needed them in my life.

It's a weird interest, but I'm a weird kid. I started researching the magnificent and ancient creatures. I was fascinated by the role reversal, the dad's did the parenting in the Emu culture. The mom would lay the clutch of eggs and once the eggs were laid, she'd hand them over to their dad. Emu moms were a lot like my mom.

None of this would convince my dad that I needed to add Emu to the family farm, but I knew what would. They were expensive! They also made good money. Folks pay well for Emu eggs. I hatched a plan.

My dad is truly part of the "man's world" and I learned a long time ago, not to appeal to his emotions. He had emotions but he wasn't exactly in touch with them. Telling him I was interested in Emu farming because I missed my mom wouldn't work. I made a business plan. I used a simple template I found on Google and then created a one, three and five year plan. I put it all in a slide show to present my dad.

I was surprised how quickly he said yes, I guess he'd been looking for some way to feel more connected with me. We began researching where we could find Emu hatchlings and before we knew it, we'd found a source to start an Emu farm. I also found an important mentor.

Her name was Annie, and you could tell her anything. She'd smile and give you a side hug and reassure you no matter what. Having an elder come into my life was truly a gift. The day I'd picked up my giant emu chicks, she'd handed me a speckled cat with a stripe running down it's back which nearly matched the stripe on the Emu themselves and given me a wink, "this little fella will help with pest control in your

Emu barn, trust me." Then she'd taken a pendant carved on the front with a little Emu and strung it on a leather strap and she gave it to me. The front shimmered when I tilted it. "That's a labradorite carving, it's a little rune to give you good luck on your Emu endeavor." I thanked Annie with a bear hug and my Emu adventures truly began.

I probably texted Annie 500 times the first few months, my Emu experience was raising questions nearly every day, but as the Emu grew into adulthood, I became more confident. We spent hours together and when I was done with chores I'd linger all day, chatting with the Emu and petting my cat as he weaved in and out between my ankles. I was an expert in no time.

I would wake up early every morning, make my way to their barn, feed and water them, and then I'd stay out there all day, tending to their needs and generally just being with them. There's a certain way an Emu looks at you, childlike and kind...a but also wise and ancient. It draws you in, I could've moved into that little barn and stayed with them forever. They loved me as I was. There were no lies with the Emu family.

I'd named my cat Diggory and the two Emu were X and Y, named for their chromosomes. In order to make sure you get a mating pair of Emu, you have to do genetic testing. Their first identity the day I picked them was as XX and XY Hatch 3, spring 2019. Annie kept impeccable records of her Emu endeavor and she encouraged me to do the same.

The days since bringing X, Y and Diggory home had been super busy and filled with joy for me. I spent less and less time at home masking for my dad, and more and more time outdoors, being my true self with the Emu family. Whatever their chromosomes, Emu were amazing creatures who embraced diverse roles within their flock family, and I adored them deeply.

My dad stopped me as I was running out early one morning to be with the birds, "What are you doing out there for hours every day, Jimmy?"

I hesitated, I hardly recognized my name lately, I'd started calling myself, Hatch, in my mind. I loved the name. When I thought of it, my thoughts would calm, and an image of a giant blue egg filled my heart. My safe place was there, with the egg my beloved Emu had emerged from. I was Hatch, the midwife to some giant feathered dinosaurs. I'd started calling myself Hatch, the day I'd walked up to the Emu couple and discovered Y in the full throws of courtship. The Emu makes a noise so strange when dancing for his lover, a kind of hollow drumming sound as though a bouncy ball was rattling in a soup can. It was an ancient sound, and X thought it was lovely. The affection between them was so pure. I wondered if it was ever like that when humans fell in love.

The day I walked out to the fields and found the Emu dancing for each other I was so excited. It was January and they were about three years old. The young couple were ready to become parents. The next two weeks were full of dancing and in a couple of days X would lay an egg in the nest she'd made for her clutch. When there were 5 eggs, she got up from the nest, and gave it to Y. He dutifully took over, spreading his feathers gently over the clutch and nuzzling the giant eggs every now and then so they gently rotated. The rolling of the eggs was an important responsibility, eggs that weren't rotated would slowly meld to the chick inside. Untested eggs were doomed. That wasn't happening to X and Y's clutch. He took over with enthusiasm, and for the next 50 days, he wouldn't even eat. Emu dads are amazing.

My excitement grew as the eggs matured. I would sit in the Emu pen for hours, maybe even for days, visiting with Y while he tended the nest. Then one morning, a out 40 days later, I arrived at the barn and plopped down in my favorite corner to keep Y company, and I heard something amazing.

There in the nest, from inside the eggs, the chicks were calling to me! I knew they'd be in the eggs for another week or more but already I could hear their voices. My heart thundered with excitement.

I started spending every waking moment with the nest. I convinced my dad that I'd lose a hefty investment if anything went wrong, and he even let me make myself a bunk in the barn. I never left the nest.

Early on day 50 I woke up to shuffling and some unusual sounds from Y. When I sat up in my bunk and looked over, I saw an egg pushed out of the nest. My heart sank. I rushed over and laid on the ground next to the egg, my cheek pressed against its smooth surface. It was silent. The chick inside had succumbed to some unknown force, and it's spark was gone.

I felt the energy go out of me as my body sagged and a sob escaped from my lips. I choked off the grief.

Boys don't cry.

That's what I told myself and then as soon as the words were in my head, the tears began to fall. I wasn't a real boy. I didn't even want to be a boy at all if that meant I wasn't allowed to be sad. I let myself cry. "It's okay to have feelings," I mumbled to myself.

The tears felt like they fell for hours, but it was probably only a few minutes later that I was able to calm down and control myself. I looked up at Y, as upset as I was, this must be harder for him. "I'm sorry we lost this one," I said softly as I sat up and looked at him.

For a moment, we made eye contact.

I felt the calm comfort in his gaze as he blinked slowly at me. Death is a natural part of life, his own thoughts flowed into mine. I knew he was right, I took a deep breath, carefully picked up the grapefruit sized egg and walked outside.

It was still a couple hours before sunrise and the cold air bit into my face. The barn was insulated and warm, it was easy to forget it was winter. I wasn't really sure what to do with the egg. I glanced around me and thought of the forests surrounding our farm. I'd take the egg to a special tree, a compass tree I'd often sit in and read, and I'd leave it there for nature. The forest would know what to do with this lost chick.

When I returned to the Emu barn it was full of activity. I'd only been gone for moments, but it could have been hours.

The eggs were pipping.

The hatching of an egg is a magical thing, and this was the first time I'd ever seen it. The chick, bursting from within, is armed with a tiny pickaxe at the end of its beak. Carefully it chips away at the egg from inside. You can hear the tap tapping as it joins with the peeping of the bird. Hours before the chick appears, a small chip appears in the shell of the egg. The chip slowly expands into a line which splits the egg almost perfectly into two, like a plastic Easter egg popped open by a toddler. If you've ever tried to peel a hard boiled egg, you know how difficult it is to control the cracking of an egg shell. The unborn chicks are given the perfect tool, and the egg unzips over the course of hours and sometimes even days. The pipping.

Within the next two sunrises, X and Y would have a family. I wanted to rush over and help the chicks along, pulling from the outside so the bird would hatch even more quickly. I resisted the urge. The best way to help any creature come into this world is to leave it alone and trust that nature knows.

I spent the next day in vigil, watching over the nest as the eggs slowly prepared to open. When it finally happened, the chicks arrived in a burst. With one final shove, one of the eggs opened and a slimy hatchling rolled into the straw. Quickly the other three did the same. The barn became loud with the sound of hungry chicks. Y and I sprang into action. The chicks cleaned their own feathers as I fetched the feed I'd prepared for this precise moment. It was rich with nutrients and would give these chicks the best start. I brought the feed and found one chick perfectly still in the nest. The other three chicks already stood on shaking and awkward legs, cleaning the gunk from their feathers. I put the food down for them and carefully approached the chick which lay on the ground. I wasn't sure what to expect from Y, we had been friends for years but that didn't mean he wanted me near his hatchlings. He dipped his head at me as I approached, a friendly gesture. I knew it was okay for me to try and help.

I quickly realized that the fourth chick had already died, it's egg still clinging lightly to one side. This little one never fully escaped the shell. I lifted it gently and took it away from the other three hatchlings, I wanted their first moments to be joyous and the lost one could change that. I nodded at Y and took the chick out into the night. I was proud of myself for not crying.

Quietly, I crept into my house and went to the bathroom sink. There, I finished cleaning the little bird and gently dried it with an old rag. Newborn chicks don't have real feathers, and when I was done, I discovered a fluffy little body that you could practically cuddle. Except this little one was dead. I wrapped it gently in a paper sheet I found and walked back to the compass tree where the egg still sat in the moonlight.

In the night skies above me, a giant vulture swooped across the face of the moon. I glanced up and shuddered a little, maybe I shouldn't leave them out here. I remembered Y's calm blinking and the thought he'd shared with me.

Death is a part of life.

I let that comfort me, placed the tiny bundle on the tree next to the egg, and walked away.

The sounds and smells of the Emu barn, now somehow brimming with the hatchlings, were delightful to my senses. The chicks were fuzzy, and demanding, and ridiculous and magical.

I was completely in love.

This was my calling. I wanted to spend every single day for the rest of my days, helping spirits be born into this life. I wanted to be a midwife. Hatch, the midwife.

The sun was finally rising and as I glanced out of the Emu barn at the display of pink and gold greeting us all, a hummingbird darted by. Then, a second hummingbird darted into view, and finally a third. The last bird paused, hovering so close to my face that I could feel the wind from its tiny wing beats.

I knew why they were here. It was time to tell my dad the truth. I took a deep breath and walked towards home.

The kitchen was quiet when I walked through the side door of our little house. I could smell coffee and hear the TV in the living room. I knew my dad was up. It was pretty early. Maybe I shouldn't interrupt his coffee, I thought to myself. I almost turned around to leave again when I heard him call.

"Jimmy is that you?" he asked.

I knew this was the moment, I knew there was a reason he'd already heard me come in. I walked into the room where he was sitting, enjoying his morning routine before a day full of work and chores. We weren't the sort of folks to sit around, and this was his quiet time. I sat down across from him, careful not to block his show.

"Dad, can we talk?" I asked, trying to start the conversation.

He turned off the TV and looked at me. I shrank a little under his gaze, "Sure, how's it going out there? Any chicks yet?"

I forgot why I was there as excitement took over, "Yeah! Last night! It was awesome, Dad. The chicks are really gross and really cute. I just love them already."

He gave me a strange look. "Jimmy, don't get attached to the chicks, they're an investment, not a friend."

I furrowed my brow in defiance, "No, they're not friends. They're practically family. They're not an investment dad, they're more than that. I'm more than that."

"What the hell are you talking about?" he let his frustration leak out.

I froze as the words became trapped behind my lips. Several heartbeats passed as I tried to find words.

I finally spoke, "Dad, I don't want to upset you, but I need to tell you something." I started the conversation again, "I know it's hard to understand, but I'm not a guy. I'm nonbinary. I don't want you to call me Jimmy anymore. I want you to call me Hatch. My real name is Hatch."

I saw the confusion settle in my dads eyes, and then the flood of anger that quickly replaced it. "You're GAY?!?" he shouted as he stood up from the chair, his coffee forgotten, "You think I raised you to run around acting gay?!?"

I summoned my courage, "You didn't raise me like this," I said, defiantly making eye contact. "I am who I am, just like anybody."

His face flushed with red as he loomed over me. I saw it in his eyes, the moment he thought about erasing me, his only child. His humiliation.

He did not strike me down, but his words cut deep as his voice boomed in the small room, "Get out of my house. NOW! My son died today."

I fled from there with the wind at my back, thinking of the look in his eyes. He'd almost killed me from shame. My stomach twisted and my legs faltered but I gathered my strength and ran until I reached the Emu barn.

The flock was there, waiting for me as though I was expected. Of course, I was expected, this was the ONE place where I was loved exactly as I was. I didn't have a plan as I'd run there, but I did now.

I pictured my dad getting his coat on and grabbing an ex from the front porch as he strode into the night. I knew he wasn't far behind me, I knew he blamed the emu for my confession.

Quickly, I grabbed an old duffel bag from the corner of the barn and started stuffing emu supplies into it. I wouldn't be able to carry much, and we'd run out quickly. I'd figure that out later.

I didn't even think of my own needs.

The moment the duffel was loaded I slung it over my shoulder and turned to my flock.

"We have to go right now," I told them, and opened the doors to the barn. In the corner, my cat stretched lazily, a giant yawn as he woke up and took in his surroundings, "You can come too, but all of you have to keep up."

I glanced around at the menagerie and headed out the door. We crossed the pasture and reached the gate which contained them all. I hesitated, the moment I opened this gate, Y might take his family and abandon me. Like my dad.

I shook the fear away and looked at X and Y.

For a moment we made eye contact.

I knew they wouldn't leave me. I lifted the latch and shoved the gate wide open.

The seven of us strode into the forest. I didn't know where we were going, but I knew I was done with humans.

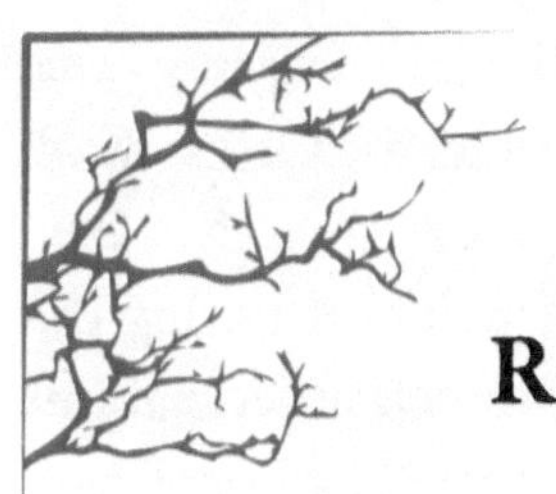

Road Side Service

Everyone loves a hard worker. Everyone admires a healer. Everyone celebrates the cycle of life.

These thing are true throughout all time. There are also other, more difficult truths to accept. The hard work might be ugly. The healing might look a lot like dying. The cure may even be death. Will the world ever celebrate the cycle of death? They will not.

That's the hard truth about the work I do. Every day, I travel this Earth finding recently departed spirits. I carefully clean their remains and prepare them for the journey they must take. I carry a part of their spirit until it can be joined with the One spirit which unites all living things. I have done this work for eons. I help their energy carry on.

I know my work is looked upon with disgust. The smell of death lingers on me. The very spirits I carry, they also cling, those who come close enough can feel them. They shrink away in disgust.

Dead spirits frighten and revolt the living. It's strange to me, as if the spirit itself is tainted by death. It is not, even in death the spirit stays, and that spirit needs a guide.

I am that guide.

This could almost seem like a cursed life, but when I accepted my responsibility, I was given the deep personal knowledge of how important this work is. If we death doulas fail to reach a spirit in time, they do not remain trapped here on Earth, they do not remain in some purgatory, they travel to neither heaven nor hell. If a spirit is not carried back to the One, they simply cease to exist. Imagine that, knowing that if you ever fail at your task, a spark will flicker out forever. I suppose in many ways, I love life more than any other being. I want every single spark to live on, their own light joining in an energy that flows through every dimension and through all time, the One spirit. It is truly beautiful.

Knowing this makes the drudgery more bearable. Knowing this makes the stares and the disgust that I encounter somehow less painful. I cannot explain to the living how precious they are, I can only carry them. I can only carry on with this dark task which I know truly brings light.

That's how it was that day. I knelt beside pregnant doe as she took her final breath. We were on a country road in a remote little place in central California. The doe looked at me with pain and fear and I murmured reassurances to her as her life faded. I promised I would carry them together, the doe and her child. I promised they would join the One spirit, together, and that her child would not need to be afraid.

Carefully I worked in ceremony, preparing them to cross with me. As with every spirit, as I did this work a part of them joined me. I would forever be connected to the doe and her child. I would be changed, this was also part of what I carried.

As I work, people drive by. They honk their horns and shout cuss words out their windows at me, some throw things. There I was, still young, having to learn the HARSH lesson of what it is like to be hated for who you are. Humans are so famous for that, they really are a lesser species.

I didn't think about any of that nonsense that day, though. In fact, I barely noticed the people driving by at all, the doe needed me, her fear was tangible in the air. I couldn't let her pass like that, both of us would be poisoned by that fear. I wove a protective spell as I worked. I let that settle into her spirit and felt her begin to relax as she was flooded with warmth and safety.

"Don't worry," I whispered, "the One spirit is beautiful, and you will be welcomed within it. I will carry a part of you forever, so that you can watch over your loved ones still here on Earth."

I saw the understanding in doe's eyes as she let go and her spirit joined mine. I did not see the maroon truck, driven by a man with a bright red, angry face, swerving towards us both. I leapt into the air carrying the doe and her child, but I was not quick enough, the truck slammed into my legs and sent my directly into the ditch where doe had just died.

I lay there gasping and trying to orient myself. I tried to find my legs, but it was as if they'd been sheared off when the truck hit me. I frantically felt for them. They were still there. I wondered if I was dying and if a doula would find me in time, and then my world went dark.

I WOKE UP SLOWLY, THE dark edges of my vision gradually brightening until I could see again. I could feel my legs! They screamed in pain, and I welcomed that pain. Pain means you're still alive.

Once my awareness really returned, I was met with a horrifying realization: I was in some sort of cage. I was in a room I didn't recognize. I panicked and cried out. There was no response. I shouted again.

Suddenly the door burst open, and a child rushed in. She seemed to be about 6 or so years old, but she had a wise look on her young face. Next to her a black and grey fluffy cat with half of it's left ear missing darted through the door and sat a short ways away, staring at me.

"You're awake!" she exclaimed, excitement in her voice.

I looked all around me, almost expecting she must be talking to somebody else in the room. It was just us three. Nobody was ever, ever excited to see ME. The smell of death, my ugly face, the underlying fear that maybe I was here to gather them up, all these things fill a heart when they gaze upon me. I braced myself and looked at her calmly, waiting for the real response to my presence.

Instead of the wave of horror I'd expected her to display, the girl looked at me calmly as well.

"Do you know you were hit by a car?" she asked me as she took a slow step closer to the pen which trapped me. I stared back. "I saw you when we were driving by. My mom wouldn't stop, but I snuck back last night and checked on you. I thought you were dead, but you're not," she talked calmly in a little babble, like a quickly moving stream along ancient stones, her words tumbled out.

I watched her approaching. As much as most people were disgusted by me, I was also not a fan of most people. They're so short sighted, so selfish, so... short lived. I always looked at humans with a little scorn. In all the generations of humanity that I've watched live and die, I have never carried a human to the One spirit.

I know it sounds harsh, but humans are a lesser being, a stunted species created by Phoenix for her own entertainment. Why would I ever want one of them to become intertwined with my spirit?!? Whatever sick part of them which could not truly love the rest of creation, whatever part of them which was so limited, it could be contagious. I'd never risk my sanity like that.

This girl was different. Her voice carried a note I'd never heard in a human before. Her energy was good. I turned my head to the cat and gave him a curious glance. He gave me a knowing nod and looked meaningfully at the girl. HE was clearly a fan of this human. Cats have been enamored with humans for many generations. His feelings could only be trusted to a certain point. I looked at the girl again, she was still talking, and was now standing directly next to my cage, within reach. She had a bottle of water and some other container in her hands. I wasn't hungry yet and not feeling called to carry any spirit, but I was really, REALLY thirsty.

I vaguely thought about gouging her eyes out or ripping off a finger. I didn't want her coming so close. It was disrespectful. Instead, I backed up a little and sat down. I wanted to see if she'd give me the water.

She approached the cage calmly and bent over and filled a dish that was already in the cage. I took a drink immediately. What a relief. I was so heavy with the weight of doe and her child, I'd never been meant to carry the spirits for so long. The journey usually took moments, not hours. It was because I still had them, that I struggled so much to stay calm although my heart pounded. I had a responsibility to these spirits. I could not let them be poisoned by my fear. I took a deep breath after a long drink and peered at the girl who was now only a few inches from my face. Her eyes were a deep dark brown which shimmered red in the sunlight that peeked into the room. She had tangled blond hair spilling over her shoulder in knots and curls. She smiled at me, not once acknowledging the presence of death as it filled the air between us.

"My name is Kanik, and this is my cat, Axle," she said to me calmly. "We are you're friends. I want to help you get better," she hesitated for a moment, "I'm sorry if this hurts, I used it on my chickens, and it helped them heal."

I looked at her and started to say something but before I could, she reached into the cage with her other hand and sprayed whatever was in the container all over my legs! I shouted with the pain that flooded my body and for a moment I could barely see. I angrily moved away and cussed her out loudly.

She shrank back from the cage and waited for me to calm down and when the flash of hot pain finally died, I was able to calm my voice as well.

She filled the silence with her babbling again, "I'm sorry that hurt so much, humans never stop to think if our medications might be painful for animals. We hardly consider animals at all," she said. She tilted her head at me and began to chatter away about her thoughts on humanity, nature, the universe... her trickle of words running all the way to the sea of thoughts that obviously filled her young mind. I listened to them while I brooded and stared at her and slowly, I faded off to sleep, too tired to stay vigilant. My last thought was of freedom as sleep stole my will away.

We continued on like that for many days. I couldn't tell you how many, it could have been three days or three hundred days. Some hours passed as quickly as a heart beat and some so slowly it seemed as though all the world must have stopped spinning. The captivity was torment and inside my spirit I could feel the mother and her child reeling with confusion and fear. Nobody knew what awaited after death, but they knew THIS was not right. I knew this was not right, and so did Kanik. I listened to her babbling for hours and those were the quick and merciful hours, the ones which flew by. Then a noise or a change in energy and Kanik would startle and run for the door. I began to realize that this little one lived a tormented life. I was in a cage, but so was Kanik. A cage made of fear and anger. The trap so complete that she would not walk away even though her body appeared free. How sad for little Kanik. She'd sometimes come in limping or clutching at her tummy in odd ways. Those days as soon as she sat, Axle hopped in her lap and nuzzled and purred and tried to use his own small magic to heal little Kanik. He couldn't stop the torment in her life, but because of his efforts, her heart did not harden. Kanik had the spirit of a healer, and Axle worked diligently to protect that. I began to secretly adore the little dyad. If only Kanik would free me, I could maybe even love them. I didn't understand why she refused to free me.

The day things shifted, I was there as always when little Kanik came in, she was in good spirits and apologized and applied the medicine quickly and perched on her favorite spot to tell me stories of her day. The thing about these stories, they were so full of little Kanik's world and her thoughts on her world, as if the door was thrown open to see her reality. Yet always, something lurked. The things she did not say. The stories she did not tell. As much as I began to care about Kanik, I also despised this weakness. How could she turn her own mind from the truth? How could she weave lies in her own heart to cover the monstrous reality which was obviously her life? Why did she never unlock the damn cage?!?

I finally reached a breaking point. After hours, or weeks, or months in that box with Kanik spinning her tales and never once facing her truth, I think I lost my mind. I just started screaming at her, and her body went stiff, and her eyes stopped blinking and she sat there and stared at me and FINALLY she saw that we were both monsters. I kept screaming until my voice rose out of that cage and that building and resonated throughout the universes. I was every trapped spirit in that moment, I was even Kanik, herself.

When I screamed, the door to the building suddenly burst all the way open and a tall man stepped in. He was such an immense figure he nearly blotted out the sunlight behind him. My eyes were still adjusting to the startling change in light and my screams barely stopped when he filled the room with his own yelling.

"What the HELL did you bring in here?!? I told you to stop dragging nasty things back to this property!" he shouted as he strode into the room, stepping on Axle as he did and snatching little Kanik up like a rag doll. She dangled a couple feet off the ground, and he angrily shook her, she shouted out in pain, and he got louder, "quit acting like a baby!" The man screamed and then I watched in horror as he tossed her against the wall. She crumpled to the ground and curled into a little ball, quietly trying to make herself invisible. He picked her up again and walked out of the room, her body dangling in resistance or fear. She was very quiet as the door slammed loudly behind them.

I stood there stunned as the room settled from the awful things that had unfolded. Axle peered out from the corner where he'd found a deep dark space to hide. I looked at him and shook my head sadly, "Is it always like this?" I asked. Axle nodded at me, and I felt his fear and grief.

Our conversation was interrupted by the screams. Somewhere, little Kanik was being tortured. I looked at Axle and he looked back,

"I've got to get the hell out of here!" I said, flooded with anger. I wanted to find a way to stop him from hurting her. Axle agreed and then, surprisingly he went over, stood on his hind legs, and slid the latch out of the locked position. It fell away easily.

"They used to use this on me, they don't know I broke it," he told me. "Please don't leave until you help her."

I burst out of the cage and directly past Axle towards the door. Quickly I discovered that when the man slammed the door it had bounced back open, leaving it slightly ajar. I rushed through and found myself outside a small barn and adjacent to some kind of work shop. The cries of pain continued from inside. I flew to them, fury propelling me directly towards the sounds and there I saw him standing over her tiny form. Without a chance to plan what I'd do I slammed my entire body into him and knocked him to the ground. Angrily I clawed at his face and arms, letting my rage guide my actions into a storm that overwhelmed him. Behind me I heard Kanik running, her footsteps fading rapidly as she escaped her living nightmare. I didn't stop until the man was still. I would make sure he didn't hurt her again.

When he passed, I saw his corrupted spirit thrashing around looking for a way to continue on, and then flicker into the abyss.

Good.

True death for humans like him, as long as humans like him are around, humanity will be lost.

I left that blighted land and rushed towards the One spirit. The doe and child had become so heavy. I flew swiftly, afraid if I didn't get them home soon, I wouldn't be able to carry on with my work. My mind stayed on Kanik and Axle. We were connected now, not like when I carried the dead, this was something different. We saved each other. When I had time, I'd be back.

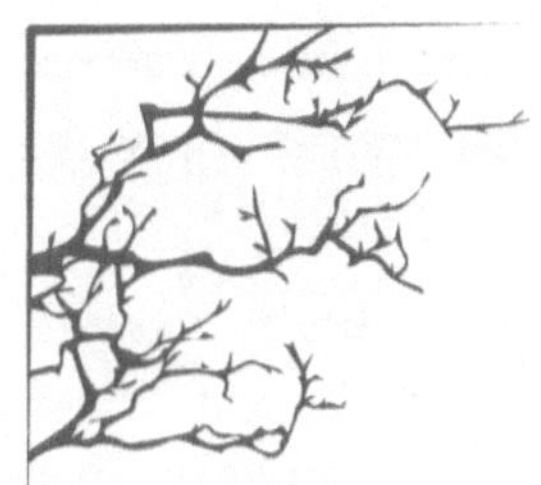

The Lovers

In a time before memory, there were the birds. They were vast beings who traveled through the multiverse on wings propelled by magic. They were not burdened by many things. Birds live on through their own hatchlings, and their spirits are nearly immortal. Though the average bird might travel through an incomprehensible distance of time and space, all birds returned to just one place when it was time to nurture a clutch. They returned to the nesting planet, Earth. The smallish planet rotating the perfect distance from a certain sun in the Milky-way galaxy was the one habitat where every bird could build its nest. Their lives were ideal, and the birds lived in harmony.

Except for the Phoenix.

Unlike the other spirits, Phoenix had been directly entrusted with magic. Phoenix was the Fire Keeper. She was guilty of great vanity amongst the sky spirits because of this gift, and openly wanted to rule the others. There was no such necessity for the spirits to be ruled over, so they laughed and teased her for her annoying flaw.

"Phoenix, would you like a creature to rule over?" asked Owl. (It was before the time of first names).

"I deserve it! Why be given such magic to sit around and do nothing?" she answered vehemently.

The council murmured.

"Perhaps we could give you a pet?" offered Hawk.

"A pet? Don't mock me!" spat back Phoenix.

"What if it was more than a pet?" suggested Hen. She was the wisest of the spirits.

"How so?" asked Phoenix. She trusted Hen, loved her, even.

"We'll help you create a magical species that is much like ourselves, capable of love and learning, but limited, so that they'll always be grateful for your leadership and guidance," suggested Lark.

"With what shall we create these pets and how should we limit them?" inquired Hawk.

"Let's create them with this very earth we live upon, and limit them by holding them bound to it, moving about awkwardly on their feet," suggested Hen.

"Let's put a tiny bit of your own magic, a spark, in each of their hearts, unlike us, they will each have a separate and limited soul," added Eagle.

"Then I'll put a craving for the fire in them, so that they are ambitious like I am. I'll guide that ambition to great futures for us all!" agreed Phoenix.

"This will be good," came the murmurs of the council.

That was how they created humans.

The Council looked over them, pleased with the design.

"We should have given them feathers," laughed Crow, "for the rest of time I'll taunt them for their nakedness."

"Why have feathers if you cannot fly?" asked Seagull. "I'll talk about their failings every time I see them and steal away their treasures."

"They may not fly but their hearts will still soar, like my heart when I waddle about the tree top nests far from the ocean. My spirit will never be as awkward as my body," said Murrelet.

"I like them. As long as they defer to my superiority, I'll even love them," beamed Phoenix.

Over time, many things changed.

The humans scrabbled out of the dark and they began forcing the world around them to be created in THEIR image and not the image of Phoenix. They got arrogant and dangerous ideas, and within Phoenix a spark of jealousy was kindled. She started to consider destroying her pets. She was bored, and they were insubordinate.

Without her knowledge, the Council gathered. All of them shared concerns about the Phoenix and her jealousy turned into anger. What would they do? In their dismay, none of them noticed that Hen was not among them.

Hen asked Phoenix to go for a walk on that fated council day.

"Let's go to the sea and talk about these fiery humans of yours," she suggested to Phoenix.

"Sure," Phoenix agreed.

They glided along the bluffs overlooking the ocean and talked.

"Why have you become so jealous of the humans and their ideas?" asked Hen.

"They lust after fire," replied Phoenix.

"And if they succeed in creating fire?" asked Hen.

"The fire belongs to me," growled Phoenix as the two of them landed on a towering bluff.

"What if they do great things with it?" suggested Hen.

"Never," her flames raged higher, "I'll destroy every last one of them first," promised Phoenix.

"You'd destroy a part of yourself?" gasped Hen.

"Without hesitation, if it were growing like a disease," replied Phoenix.

"What happens if you do that? You could destroy us all!"

For a moment they made eye contact.

Hen was disgusted and very saddened. Although Phoenix had always been a flawed spirit, Hen loved her deeply, and although Phoenix had never really understood it, the two of them were twin spirits. Hen was a reflection of Phoenix, and for all the fire that raged openly in Phoenix, hidden within Hen there was an entire ocean of calm. Today Hen let go of that calm. She looked at Phoenix and saw nothing but rage and in a panic of personal weakness, she let a storm break loose.

Behind Phoenix, the ocean went dark and as they stood at an impasse, the Earth went silent, and then awoke with a rumble.

Phoenix didn't even blink or turn towards the angry quake of Hen's spellcasting. She did not see the ocean suck away, and in upon itself. She did not see the tsunami raging towards her.

She and Hen only saw each other.

"I love you," said Hen and leapt upwards off the ledge.

"I love you," answered Phoenix, as the wave swept over her, choking the fire that was her life, sucking her into its clutches and out to sea.

The ashes of Phoenix settled at the bottom of the Pacific ocean like so much meteor dust. Drowned too deeply to ever rise again, for the rest of time, the Phoenix would yearn for life. Her attempts to be born again, visible as little volcanic island chains all over the Earth.

From above, Hen looked on in horror. What had she done?!?! She reeled as the steam rose.

It was murder.

She rushed to the Council, distraught with grief and guilt. She told them all what she'd done. She told them of the way she'd murdered Phoenix.

"We should kill Hen, too," suggested Crow, "and then kill the humans ourselves. Phoenix was right, they're a plague species."

Hen quivered in fear.

"We should spare her but kill the humans," was the Starling's response. The Starling and Crow had both hated the humans from the beginning, they thought the entire thing was an indulgence of Phoenix's giant and flawed ego, and they were eager for the experiment to be over.

"Never!" interrupted Eagle. "This is the first time any of us has died. We'll not make this tragedy worse by snuffing out another precious soul."

"What then?" asked Hawk, "Reparations? How does Hen possibly pay proper penance for a crime such as this?"

They all looked at Hen.

"Let's cast her into servitude to her precious humans," suggested Crow.

"Another cruel idea from you!" Owl said scornfully, "your character gets more questionable every day. We should be asking ourselves how can we help Hen to heal? She's obviously ripped asunder from grief."

"Sometimes penance is healing," contemplated Eagle aloud, "What do you think, Hen?" she asked.

Hen quivered and looked up at the Council.

"I'm so deep in grief I cannot find my own heart. Kill me."

They all murmured again, and small argumentative conversations sprung up all amongst the sky spirits.

They'd never had to make such an awful decision.

Finally, after much debate, Eagle and Owl hushed the frantic chatter.

"We've come to a decision, we would like to see if the Council agrees," began Eagle.

"This is the greatest betrayal in memory. Done from perhaps the greatest moment of desperation any of us has ever faced."

"Would you have the guts to kill your own lover to protect the rest of us? Some of us openly scorn Hen, yet she acted as a hero. Sadly, she also acted as a murderer."

"How do we reconcile those two truths?!?" she continued peering at the faces of the on looking council members.

"Owl and I believe that Hen should indeed be sentenced to an eternity of servitude to these humans. Her daughters will be their captive slaves, seeing their eggs sacrificed to the endless human appetite. Her sons will be plucked up at birth and ground into pulp to feed those same evil cravings.

"The humans shall not know that the captive birth-waters within those eggs they eagerly devour, are actually dousing their own inner spirit-flames. In each generation, only enough sons will survive to continue Hen's spirit and guarantee her penance lasts for all of eternity, helping us dampen the fiery ideas of these dangerous humans."

Eagle finished speaking.

Silence stretched for what seemed a hundred heartbeats. In unison the silence was broken as the Council cast it's vote in a sad chorus.

"We agree."

Hen's fate was decided.

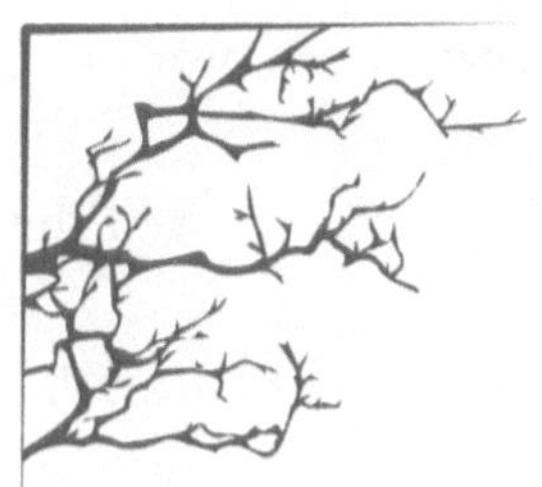

Carrier

There are certain moments and certain changes in life that you can never take back. Whatever else happens in your future, those days will stay in your heart, and you'll always think about them.

That's how it is, to be a homeless kid.

One day I was there at the giant cold house, surrounded by a family that hardly saw me, and the next moment, I was just another homeless Portland teen surrounded by a society that hardly saw me.

I'd walked out of our neighborhood and through the security gate with a casual wave. I often took a bus to the neighborhood branch of our library to check out books. This time, when I got on the bus, I didn't get back off at the library. I just kept riding until I reached a TriMet park and ride station. I transferred to a Max train and headed towards the heart of downtown Portland. I had no plan.

I realized I was in trouble a couple hours before sunset. Up until then, I'd been wandering, enjoying my freedom and the chaos of the city. The sky here didn't get much darker, the glow of the buildings and the streetlamps and the headlights on the road kept the world illuminated. Unlike the sun, none of those lights was warm. Quickly, a chill set into my bones. I pulled the hood of my sweatshirt up and wrapped my arms around my stomach, trying to hold in some of my heat. When a bus passed by, I hopped on it. Luckily my jerk of a dad always bought me annual youth passes. I could ride for free, for probably hundreds of miles around the Portland metro area. I mumbled something to the driver, found a seat with a little personal space, and settled in. I'd just sit here for awhile and figure out what to do next. I didn't even feel myself drifting off to sleep.

When I woke up, a TriMet security officer was standing over me. I startled and sat stiffly in my seat.

"What's up with you, kid? You've been on this bus for most of the route." He demanded.

I blinked off the fog of sleep and shrugged at him casually, "I'm supposed to get off in a couple more stops. I'm on the way to my mom for the weekend," I lied. "Thanks for waking me up so I didn't miss it."

He furrowed his brow, but he seemed to believe me and walked back up the aisle towards a spot by the driver. I hopped off the bus at the next stop. I'd messed up by drawing attention to myself. I hoped he'd forget me, just write me off as another idiot teen wandering the city.

It was late and I was now in a suburban area similar to where my dad lived, but on a completely different side of Portland. I didn't know the neighborhood but wandered in the general direction of some houses and away from a strip of auto dealerships. A few blocks away, I found myself in a small park with a unique fountain at its center. All around the fountain were pigeons fluttering too and fro, making a ruckus and demanding treats from a very old man who sat on a bench nearby. He talked to them like close friends, and they seemed to feel similar. I stood and watched for a long time. Finally, I found a seat next to the man.

His hand paused in the air as he tossed a little piece of berry and looked at me, "You shouldn't really feed them bread. It's not good for them. Real fruit, nuts, seeds, and veggie scraps are better. They like it just as much."

I smiled at him, I liked how he talked to me. He seemed warm and good, like my mom. "Okay. I don't have any of those things, though. Bread, either."

"Oh, I see. Want to toss them a piece or two?" He asked and held out an old butter tub with an assortment of bird-friendly treats in it.

"Yeah!" I was excited and grabbed a big handful.

He held up his hand to stop me, "Hold on, just a little at a time. If you make them work for it, you can train them to do all kinds of neat tricks."

"Really?" I asked, amazement clearly showing in my voice.

"Yes, it's late, but if you meet me here tomorrow, I'll show you all the cool things these guys know how to do." He winked at me, not a creepy wink, more like a magical elf might wink after they promised to teach you a spell.

"I'll be here!" I promised him. We sat there quietly after that, tossing tidbits and listening to the Pigeons babble.

Eventually he stood up, tucked the butter tub in an old robe he was wearing, and gave me a farewell nod, "My name's Kent, I'll see you tomorrow. Have a nice evening."

It was just me and the pigeons... but not really, because only moments later they all took off, flying after him up a nearby street and out of sight in the dark. I sat in the quiet and the cold crept back in. I'd forgotten while I was with the man and his birds, but it was a cold spring day, and the chill was brutal. I looked around, saw a play tunnel on the climbing structure and climbed up into it. I lay there and thought about the sweet old man and the pigeons. I was miserable, but I had something to look forward to.

The morning seemed a lifetime away but finally the sunrise tinted the air pink and then in a rush, the sun was up. I was so relieved, there in the tunnel it warmed up quickly and I dozed off for a bit when the chill finally let go of my bones. The sound of kids climbing the play structure woke me abruptly. I sat up and scrambled out quickly, hoping nobody had seen me asleep in there.

Sitting on the same bench, the old man gave me a familiar smile and a wave as soon as I emerged. He patted the bench next to him and I plopped down. I noticed more about him today, he was a weather worn person, everything from his eyes to his shoes told a story and the story was not gentle. Yet, beyond that thick skin and scarred heart, a genuinely warm spirit shone through. He was the sort to bring warmth and love even if he'd only ever felt the cold. A healer. I was glad to see him again.

"Good morning," I greeted him, "will you show me some of the tricks now?"

"Yes, I will," he answered, "the flock seems to be in good spirits today." He gestured towards the pigeons surrounding the bench we sat on. "First things first, I've got to pop off a message to my buddy." I sat there waiting, expecting the guy to get a phone out of his pocket, and instead he trilled at the birds. It was a weird sound that I'd not heard any bird or person make, but it was clearly familiar to one of the pigeons who immediately perked his head up and came to see us. I was shocked to discover; he was wearing a little backpack. Kent reached in his pocket, pulled out a tiny notebook and scribbled a short message on it:

Maria, I've found myself alive again this morning!
How wonderful is that?
I'm also very lucky to make a new friend, a young fella named Benji.
We and the birds all hope you have a magical day.
~Kent

He rolled the little letter into a tiny scroll, unscrewed a lid from the pigeon's tiny backpack and slipped it in. With a quick twist, the message was ready for delivery. The bird flew off at once, eager to do its duty. I sat there and watched the entire routine in amazement.

"Whoa, where does he take the message?" I asked Kent.

"He'll take that to my friend, Maria. He's flown the same route for years. She lives about an hour from here. It gives us something to do." Kent looked off towards the north and joy sparkled in his eyes.

"That's so cool. Can I send a message?" I thought Kent and the pigeons were amazing.

"Well, we can send an update tomorrow. Sometime later today our pigeon friend will bring us a message from Maria. I'll let you write the next message." Kent agreed.

The two of us spent several days like that. I think Kent secretly knew I was living at the playground. He'd bring food for me, and for the birds. It was the first time in my life that I felt accepted, there with the birds and the little old man and a stomach full of veggies. The cold nights and the dirty clothes and the yearning for my mom were all more bearable because of Kent and his birds. Whatever else happened, I had a friend. One of the days, Kent's carrier pigeon came back early, it was only about lunch time. He read the little note inside and laughed, then gave me a funny look.

"Do you want to try sending a message to someone?" he asked me.

"Oh, I don't have any friends to send it to," I shrugged, Kent was my only friend.

"If you don't have a specific friend, you just send it off like a message in a bottle. Write the letter to the universe, maybe somebody will find it, maybe somebody will write back." He gave me a reassuring wink.

"Okay sure, I'll try it." I took the little paper he was offering and scrawled a quick letter:

My name is Benji, and this is my bird.
If you find him, send a message back!
PS, his name is Wilson.
~ Benji

"Wilson?" he asked, giving me a funny look.

"Yeah, he looks like a Wilson, don't you think?" I asked him, "I'm sorry, does he have a name already?"

"No," Kent laughed, "I never name the birds, they don't need a human name."

"Well, I am going to call him Wilson, after a friend I had a long time ago... if that's okay?" I thought it would be easier for me to keep the birds apart from each other, if I named them.

"Sure, kid, Wilson it is." He nodded in agreement. I tucked the letter inside Wilson's pack, and he flew into the sky, searching for a recipient.

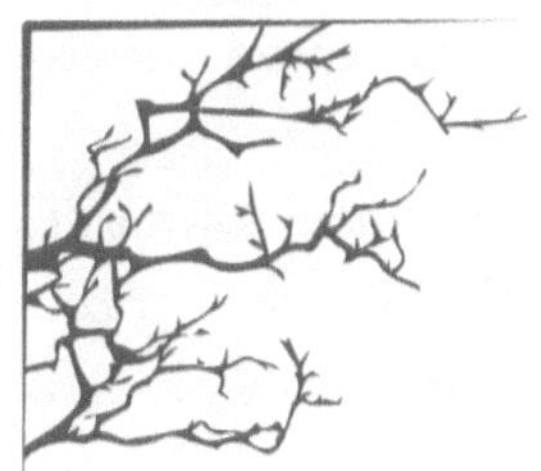

Raisins

The days after Phoenix abandoned humans were bad for the young species. Humanity had a strange custom of building habitats in places that simply weren't habitable. Cities sprang up in deserts where water had to be shipped for hours to nourish the neighborhoods. Playgrounds were built for the wealthy which provided no resource aside from human entertainment. Mega crops had taken over giant swaths of land also, crops which could not survive without the forcing of human hands. Mountain top villages clung to life in regions where bitter cold and isolation threatened for the majority of the year.

Living as they did, the humans never once questioned the safety of these communities. They had their innovations and ambitions and since recorded history, mankind had forced its will upon the Earth. There was no reason to ever think that world would end, and then it did.

The day the Phoenix abandoned them, the spark of electricity which propelled nearly all human technology, died. Airplanes fell from the sky. Cellphones became tiny plastic bricks. Cities went dark and screens went silent.

The humans had thought their sciences were the secret to their success, when all along, the secret had been the spark, given to them by the Phoenix. It was not a promise, it was a gift and when the humans betrayed her, she took it back. She was like an angry parent disconnecting the internet, except her children were all humans.

The cities fell first. They'd been weakened by Covid and then by riots and when the electricity died, people lost their minds. Within weeks, most cities were reduced to rubble. There was no slow decline, one moment everything was normal, and then in one season, massive ghost towns dotted the globe.

The very little and very isolated towns went next. Small town folks are rugged but only a few were prepared when the 45 minute trip to grab supplies in a car, turned into a two day journey through a blizzard. Many little communities struggled on in spite of the new challenges. Then the summer of 2023 happened. There was a new strain of Covid, and it spread much faster than the news of the danger. Humans had become very isolated since the lights went out. Supply missions sent from small towns into nearby suburbs returned with the virus and most people died within days.

The suburbs survived.

They managed to limp along by gathering resources from nearby farms and abandoned cities. They were often perched in places where humans could scratch out enough nourishment to keep going.

Within the suburbs, groups of people still struggled with isolation, disease, hunger... and the constant threat of birds.

There was a lot of change for humans after 2020, and one of those changes was the appearance of NEW birds. There were many who'd never been seen by human eyes, having abandoned their nesting grounds for generations, disgusted by the filth wrought by humans. These ancient beings were thrilled to return to Earth, to build nests, and to hunt humans.

Griffin and Haedi were suburban kids growing up in a community haunted by one of these newly returned avian beasts. The forest nearby was now the favorite habitat and hunting ground of a Roc. The Roc were massive birds who looked a lot like an eagle. The wing of one could span the length of a school bus and the beast itself was as big as a football field. When they flew overhead the sky darkened like a cloud passing in front of the sun. The screams of the Roc assault the ears, reminiscent of the sound of a plane breaking the sound barrier, according to some of the elders. The Roc were big enough to easily pick up and eat a cow, but they preferred humans.

Humans were given the flame by Phoenix, and they were also given her protection. A magical contract that prevented any bird from harming a human. When Phoenix abandoned humans, she left them vulnerable to anybody who wanted them. The Roc wanted them.

Roc hunt at sunrise and when the first attack happened, nobody saw it coming. There was a flicker of the sun, like a child messing with a light switch, and then the Roc snatched Jeremy the mailman up, right in the middle of town square. Witnesses who'd been up early preparing for their days, screamed and ran for cover. Quickly the word spread.

Giant birds. Hunting humans.

The little suburb, already isolated, became trapped in place. Every morning the attacks came, and the humans learned to only leave the shelter of their homes in the dead of night or the heat of day. That was when the Roc would rest.

The town slowly became more desperate, and they called a meeting at high noon on July 4th, 2037. They would find a way to stop the Roc. The folks gathered onto the bleachers of a giant old rec center gymnasium. The gym, built in the 1990s, had giant mirrored windows along one side. The lighting was good, and they could see the Roc if somehow they were attacked during the napping hours.

The meeting began but before anybody could speak, a stranger walked into the room. The Alkonost. She had a body covered in soft metallic black feathers which glistened almost like an oil slick in the sunlight. She was tall and thin and looked at them with a kind face which was sculpted from ebony skin. She was the most bewitching woman they'd ever seen. Breathtaking.

The gathered humans were struck silent with shock when the Alkonost began to sing. The music seemed to light her from within, and although her feathers were so dark, a glow emanated from her very being.

The song was a trap.

If you've ever had a treat, knowing it was nearly poison. If you've ever craved a drug, knowing it was truly poison. If you ever longed for a lover who already brutalized your heart. That was this song.

The words were tainted but the enchantment wrapped them in a spell that the humans could not resist. The Alkonost would save them from the Roc, it would simply cost them everything. The enchantress presented the humans with a magical agreement that they couldn't possibly resist. She'd woven her trap so tightly, they didn't even see it closing.

They simply had to agree to bring her two children, two times a year, and the rest of the town would be saved. The children would be her pets or her prey, it was no concern of theirs.

It would be normal for any community to be enraged at the very evil of Alkonost's offer but the towns people were lost in enchantment. One by one they floated to the feet of their feathered guest, where they groveled for her approval. They signed the children away without a second thought.

The day of the first sacrifice arrived quickly, and the people gathered again. They devised a simple lottery, placed the children's names into a hat, and chose two.

Griffin and Haedi.

The two were siblings and when they'd discussed the lottery the night before, they'd decided to write both their names on both lottery slips.

"If we go, we go together," Griffin reassured his little sister. He never once imagined that the two of them would be chosen.

The family returned home stunned and frantic. The two children would be taken at sunrise, left in a place chosen by Alkonost, and never return.

They had no way of knowing if the children would live or die, they only knew that this was their last night together.

Their father spoke first, "We could leave tonight. We just have to find shelter during the hunting hours, so the Roc don't pick us off."

"We can't," their mom shook her head as tears fell. "We signed the contract just like everyone else. If we don't take them, they'll die anyway, and the Roc will go back to hunting us all."

The children cowered in the corner while the adults discussed their fate. Terror clung to Haedi, her eyes were wide and darting. She took tiny rapid breaths and little gagging noises came from her throat.

Griffin knew she was having a panic attack. He took her right hand and squeezed firmly in the pad between her index finger and thumb. He leaned in close and whispered so only Haedi could hear, "I see the sink, my shoes, and this silly sweater you always wear. What do you see?" He asked her.

Her breathing slowed a little while her eyes darted around, "I see your hand, the wood floors, and the trees outside," she answered.

"I hear the wind, and Mom's voice, what do you hear?" He asked in reply.

"I hear Dad yelling, and I hear the birds." She smiled a little when she answered this time.

"I smell lemon cleaner, what do you smell?" Griffin kept going.

"I smell your nasty dog breath and not much else," Haedi giggled, and the worst of the panic ebbed from her mind.

"Haedi, look at me," Griffin urged her. She peered at him while their parents argued on "I have a plan, and no matter what happens, I'm going to keep you safe."

Relief flooded Haedi and she hugged Griffin tightly. She believed him.

Their parents argued for awhile but eventually they accepted the truth. This was their last night with the children. They tucked them into their own bed where everyone could gather, and they watched as the children drifted off to sleep. Finally, after watching the two peacefully resting for what seemed like hours, the parents also drifted off to sleep. Their dreams were tormented.

Griffin, who had waited patiently for his moment of opportunity, did not sleep. He went back into the front entry, where earlier that day he's seen a basket of old cellphones sitting forgotten on a shelf. Plastic bricks.

He gathered the phones, took them to the back patio, and smashed them into sparkly little pieces in the moonlight. He swept the pieces up and tucked them into the pouch pocket of his hoodie. He wasn't lying when he told his little sister he had a plan. He went back into the bedroom and saw his sleeping family. He wondered what it was like before the bird wars. He wondered what it was like to feel safe. He climbed in with them and let sleep steal his stress away.

The town had decided that no parent could really be trusted to leave their child alone in the forest for a monster to gather up, so they'd chosen a sacrifice guide. He was a younger man named Ethan with no kids of his own, he wouldn't have to take his family to be offered to Alkonost. He came for Griffin and Haedi very early. They would set out at sunrise during the dangerous hours when Roc was known for hunting. They were protected by their agreement with Alkonost.

Ethan tried to keep a rapid pace, but Griffin hesitated over and over again, slowing them all down. Ethan was frustrated, "If we're not there when the Alkonost comes, this will all be for nothing. Hurry up!" his agitation grew as the pace faltered. "Maybe you're a coward, and you don't care if everyone dies because you were too afraid to walk?" Ethan dug at him.

Griffin didn't respond. He wasn't a coward, but he didn't plan to give up without a fight. Every time he faltered, he sprinkled pieces of the phone along the path. Glancing behind him, he could see them sparkling in the sunlight.

The trail home.

Eventually they arrived at the spot where the children would be sacrificed. It seemed as if they'd walked for hours, and their legs ached from the journey. The three of them sat next to a giant serpentine boulder and Ethan handed them some water in small bottles. These bottles had probably been reused a hundred times, after machines stopped working people got really good at reusing every resource.

The kids were famished and drank every drop. Immediately Griffin started to feel dizzy and wanted to question Ethan. He never uttered a word, the sedative he'd drank kicked in rapidly and he and Haedi fell asleep where they sat.

They awoke several hours later, in the heat of the late afternoon. There was no sign of Ethan or of Alkonost. The children stumbled to their feet and then Griffin gestured for Haedi to keep quiet and follow him into the cover of the trees. They crouched under a giant bush and Haedi clung to him in fear.

Griffin shook off the cobwebs in his mind, the sedative still clung and made his thoughts sluggish and disjointed. He whispered at Haedi, "I left us a trail so we can find our way home," he pointed towards his left, there in the afternoon sunlight the pieces of glass and plastic shimmered. The fragments of old phones he'd scattered as they walked would guide them. Haedi spotted them and started towards the path, relieved to get away from the sacrifice spot. Griffin reached out and held her back by her shoulder, "We're not going to walk directly down the trail, he whispered. We have to be careful, anything could be waiting."

For a moment, they made eye contact.

They thought about Ethan, the Roc, Alkonost. It was a dangerous forest. The two of them crept along silently, staying under bushes and out of sight of the skies. They continued to walk for the rest of the day and just as Griffin began to worry, they'd lose sight of the sparkling trail in the dark, the forest became familiar.

They were almost home! They rushed forward and as they approached the broken-down sidewalk that led to their neighborhood, the sun went down. They snuck home in the moonlight.

When the two of them walked into their house, both parents gasped with shock and rushed to them. They wrapped them in hugs and tears of relief.

They didn't know what would happen tomorrow but for tonight they were together. It felt like magic.

THERE WAS AN ANGRY mob at the door early the next morning. The family huddled together as the door rattled from fists pounding. The community wanted answers. Their dad frantically grabbed a box of commodity raisins and two quarts of water and shoved them into Griffin's sweatshirt.

"Hide this food, and don't eat anything they give you! They're probably going to try and drug you again," he looked at them both in earnest, "Don't defy them. Say thank you and pretend to eat. Do NOT swallow, you need to keep your wits, or you'll never have a chance out there. Do you understand?" He asked them hastily.

The children nodded numbly as their parents ushered them to the door. Quickly they were amongst the mob, being swept into the forest again. The angry townspeople shouted insults at the children.

"How dare you come back here!?"

"You could have killed us all!"

"What a couple of cowards!"

The children withered under the insults as they marched on. They walked much farther this time and in the center of the angry crowd they couldn't tell where they were going.

Griffin hatched a plan. He thought of the cell phone pieces that had led them home the day before, and he started stealthily dropping raisins as he walked. He and Haedi would follow them home, just like last time. This time they'd be smarter and find a way to escape with their parents before the villagers came for them again.

They reached a hillside and scattered about it were massive boulders, and piles and piles of bones.

"What is this?" Haedi asked, fear tinged in her voice.

Ethan, who was there again that day, gave the children an angry look, "Alkonost is angry about your betrayal, and she doesn't want you anymore. She told us to feed you to the Roc, and next month we can try again to provide a worthy sacrifice and treaty.

The two children cowered in terror. Their fate was no longer unknown. They'd both been there the day Jeremy was ripped to shreds and swallowed. They would be eaten. Griffin hugged his little sister tightly and tried not to let his fear show.

"You're no different than the monsters, if you'd leave us here to die. A snack for the beasts so that you can save your own skin. Do any of you even deserve to live if you could do such a thing?" He asked them defiantly.

"We only want to live. We don't have a choice." Ethan said sadly.

"You'd live a life like this? A waking nightmare? I guess I'd rather die." Haedi said, bravery seized her spirit.

"You'll be getting what you desire, then." Ethan replied, "I've brought you some lunch. Eat this food and we'll leave you to your fate."

"This isn't OUR fate." Griffin said angrily as he accepted the food. The moment he had a chance he ground all of it into crumbs and scattered it about the hillside. He and Haedi pretended to eat with enthusiasm and when they were done, they put on the performance of their young lives.

"I'm so tired," Haedi yawned and slumped against a boulder, little snores escaping her nose from time to time.

"I'm tired too," Griffin agreed, and he stretched out on the ground next to Haedi and lay perfectly still.

The townspeople didn't linger for long. They were terrified of the Roc and left the sleeping children to their fate.

Griffin sat up as soon as he and Haedi were alone. "Haedi, quickly, we have to get out of here before the Roc wakes up from his nap."

The two of them stood up and glanced around. Massive skulls from cows and moose dotted the hillside. The Roc could eat either of them in one quick swallow. They hurried out of the area and towards the direction they'd come from.

Griffin scanned the ground for raisins. His heart began to thunder as he glanced around and saw nothing. He did not know that Crow, forever antagonizing the scourge of humanity, had stolen the raisins away and eaten them.

Crow knew something that all birds knew and that somehow humans did not. There are lines you can cross as a species and as a spirit that you can never come back. Like a bell, once rung, the waves reverberate forever: sacrificing your own children is one of those lines.

Crow was thrilled to see this little outpost of humans had given up on themselves so completely that they'd sacrifice their own children. The death of these two humans would be the first REAL blow against the human spirit, a trauma that couldn't be healed. Humanity wouldn't survive long after they rung this bell.

Griffin and Haedi, abandoned by their community and sabotaged by the crow, were truly lost.

"What do we do?" Haedi asked her brother.

"We just go, Haedi. We just get the hell OUT of here and we never look back." Griffin held her hand and together they walked into a line of trees nearby. It would be safer under the trees, where the Roc cannot fly.

There at the bone yard, the Roc woke from his afternoon nap and found his hillside scattered about with tiny tidbits of bread. He was tempted by the sweet smell and so he lazily combed the ground with his talons and ate as many morsels as he could find. Unknowingly he swallowed the sedative meant for the two children and dozed back off for an unexpected second nap. This little twist of fate allowed Griffin and Haedi to travel hours away from the boneyard before the Roc was awake again, giving them the lead that might save their lives.

The children moved deeper into the forest.

These forests aren't like you might imagine them, they'd become more wild when humans died in large swathes those first years of the bird wars. They'd become more chaotic and dangerous when Phoenix abandoned them, and magical birds descended. The forests were alive, and some spirits were friendly, but many were not. The children moved as quietly and quickly as they could manage, they wanted to cross through these woods before they were noticed by the spirits darting through the canopies.

They would not be so lucky. The land they were traversing was a place once called Yellowstone. This space was protected even during the height of human ambition, carefully left in its most wild state. When the power went out, these vast horizons were immediately feral again. The forest here went for hundreds of miles. Once upon a memory, tourists would take a day or even two, to wind through this wilderness in cars.

It would take Griffin and Haedi months on foot, and the birds were only one of the threats they faced along the way. They walked along with determination, not knowing the odds they faced.

The first day they were propelled by fear and hardly felt the ache of walking or hunger. They fell asleep under a thicket scattered with deer poop. Griffin had seen the wallow and realized it was a place where deer slept safely. He and Haedi curled up there trusting that the deer knew a safe place when they saw it.

Morning arrived and they began walking again, but today Haedi seemed to feel everything. She cried and whined and begged Griffin to find them food. He thought of the raisins and guilt crept up his spine. He shouldn't have tossed them down. Now they had nothing to eat. He kindly encouraged Haedi, and they took lots of breaks and kept going. He remembered to always leave one eye to the canopies. They might eventually die of hunger, but they'd immediately die if the Roc found them.

They walked for hours and then they came upon the strangest stream. It did not seem to flow. Instead of a current moving from one direction to another, it was a series of holes whose puddles ran together in a long line and appeared like a stream only until they were standing directly above it. Once they were close, they could see it behaved nothing like a stream.

Haedi looked at her brother, "What is it?"

"I don't know. Smells funny." He answered.

"I'm thirsty, can I drink it??" Haedi took a step towards the mysterious stream.

"I don't think so, don't touch it," Griffin responded as he glanced around him. He walked over to a small plant, plucked a flower off of it and tossed it into the stream.

Steam sizzled as the flower withered into a tiny wrinkled blob, "It's hot." Griffin declared.

They both took an uneasy step back as they realized what a stream like this could do to their bodies, Haedi pictured hotdogs boiling in water, and shuddered.

Looking around them, Griffin realized the super hot water was everywhere. Mud along the creek had steam subtly rising from it, and many of the plants here were different from the ones they'd seen all day. They'd walked into a surreal landscape. It was as if the earth was hot and melted just below the surface where they stood. He thought of the Phoenix.

"Haedi, I think we should go." He suggested and tugged on her arm as he headed away from the heat.

The very air around them seemed hot and as the day wore on, Griffin also became overwhelmed with hunger. He'd give nearly anything to have a raisin or two.

They were stumbling along exhausted and starving when a strange bird fluttered up and landed on a nearby branch. She looked like a small Owl, but her face was human.

Griffin paused, he knew that magical birds could be very dangerous. She smiled at him, and he was immediately enamored. He forgot his fears and smiled back. The Sirin began to sing and then flew off to a nearby tree and seemed to wait for them. The enchantment pulled them towards her, and they followed her farther into the wilderness. Soon they came to a very dense thicket and the bird flew into the brush. Without hesitation the children followed her.

BRANCHES LINED WITH angry thorns clawed at the children, but they pushed forward. The magical bird, nearly pulsing with temptation, helped distract them from the pain. Nothing mattered but the Sirin song.

They burst from the thicket's grasp and into a giant ring of fruit trees. The children's village had lived entirely on commodities that the adults foraged from a nearby city. They'd never seen such bounty, the magical trees hung heavy with their treasures and the children rushed forward, hardly noticing the tiny cabin in the center of the trees which was surrounded by vast gardens. The first thing Griffin chose was an orange, while Haedi plucked a pear from just above her head. These were no ordinary fruits, they hovered in the magical moment of perfect ripeness, and they nearly burst with juice. The children found themselves drunk with pleasure. They did not wonder where the little angel-faced owl had gone, and they did not notice the small figure which emerged from the little house and watched them eat until their sides burst.

The Ceridiwen watched them closely, thrilled that the Sirin had brought her such a treat. She could go to them in bird form and eat them now, but they were skinny. She would fatten them up, first.

She walked over in human form, appearing to them as a middle aged woman with kind eyes, "I see you found my orchard." she said, and the children both startled.

Griffin wanted to drop the fruit and instead he took another bite. He grimaced at himself. Where was his self control? He mumbled around the wedge of orange he'd just shoved in his mouth, "I'm sorry, we didn't know this belonged to somebody."

"Well of course it belongs to somebody," she laughed, a delightful sound that reminded Haedi of birdsong. "Would you like some bread and cheese to go with your fruit?" She asked them.

"Cheese?!?" The children repeated in unison. Cheese was the stuff of legends. They followed her into the little cottage without a second thought.

Inside the little house they were treated to an elaborate feast by their friendly hostess. This was the first day in many days that the children felt that things might finally be okay. It was as if they'd stumbled upon a long lost auntie.

The evening was lovely and as the sun set their hostess lit a small fire in the mantle and pulled a chest out of the corner. She began to bring a magical assortment of bedding out of the small chest, each blanket appearing as though from some bottomless source. With a final grand gesture, she presented a luxurious feather mattress from the box and placed it gently in front of the fire.

"You can rest here, you must be exhausted from your long journey." She patted the bed reassuringly.

The bed felt like floating on the pillows of a warm cloud, and the two children fell deeply asleep.

THEY WOKE IN KENNELS, separated and stacked one on top of the other. The woman was no longer in her human form but instead stood before them as her true self, the Ceridiwen. She was monstrous. A giant beast with the face of a chicken and the body of a Hawk, she looked over them.

"Who are you?" Griffin demanded.

"You don't recognize me?" she laughed, and for a heartbeat she showed him her human face again. He shrank back in the cage.

"What do you want?" He asked her, wide eyed with fear.

She laughed viciously, "I want what all birds want," she scowled, "I want you dead. I bet a couple juicy little tidbits like you will be delicious."

Haedi finally overcame her fear, "Please don't eat us. Let me help in your garden. If you let us live, I'll help you have way more food than just us two skinny kids."

The Ceridiwen considered her offer, "I'll give you three days to prove your worth. I will decide after that time, if you are better for food or field hands. I'll keep your brother in his kennel, so you aren't tempted to run."

She let Haedi out of her kennel and barked her first command at her, "Fetch the manure from the barn out back and spread it amongst the blue berries."

"How will I know which plants are the blueberries?" She asked, she'd never been in a garden before that day.

"Are you stupid?" her captor replied, "the blueberry plants have BLUE berries."

Haedi left the little cottage and went towards the barn and gardens, her cheeks burning with embarrassment. The blueberries have blue berries. How could she be so slow?

Haedi completed her first task and then her first day and then she quickly arrived at the end of the three day trial. She woke up and went to the door of her kennel to be set free. She smiled at her captor, trying to convince the wicked bird that she was a friend.

"Have you thought about our fate?" Haedi asked the Ceridiwen. She nearly held her breath waiting for a reply.

"Yes, we will discuss your fate after morning chores," she replied, "go fetch me kindling for the fire."

Haedi did as she was told but a nagging thought ran through her mind, "This is day three and today she said she'd kill us." She collected her load and stumbled back, burdened under its weight. Every day she hurt from the work she did, but that's okay she told herself. Pain means you're alive. In the hardest moments, that's how she kept going.

She came back and dutifully built a fire in the hearth.

"Stoke it up nice and hot, I'm making a feast today," she leered at Haedi and then gave her a list of ingredients, "Go fetch these from the garden."

Haedi did as she was told, and as she worked her stomach slowly tightened. She knew the monster would never let them go.

The nightmare turned into a living hell when Haedi walked back into the witch's hut. There she discovered her brother already roasting in the fire while the witch cackled and watched.

Haedi screamed in terror and rushed towards her in rage. The wicked old hag barely had time to look up when Haedi shoved her headlong into the flames.

Haedi fled the cabin, horrified by what she'd seen and gripped with grief at Griffin's death. She wanted to run and never stop running. She summoned her bravery and stopped before crossing through the magic thicket which had led them there.

She couldn't leave Griffin alone in the ashes, even if he was dead.

Haedi turned back towards the cursed cottage, took a deep breath and walked in. The stench from the fire was nearly unbearable. Burnt feathers and flesh.

She approached the dwindling fire and after reassuring herself that the Ceridiwen was definitely dead, she began the grim task of shifting through the ashes. Carefully she retrieved the smaller bones of her brother. She left the witch there to rot.

She gingerly carried her brother's bones into the garden and there she found a giant pumpkin. Carefully she hollowed out the center and placed her brother's bones inside. Then she climbed the tallest fruit tree in the garden and set the pumpkin amongst the branches. They bent dangerously under the load.

Haedi climbed down and looked up at her brother. She didn't really know why she'd done this, but she felt better. Suddenly she was overwhelmed with exhaustion and lay at the base of that very tree and fell deeply asleep.

Soon, a full moon rose above both children and the nocturnal spirits began their dance. Somehow, somewhere in the night, one of those spirits took pity on Griffin. She decided to weave a little magic.

The next morning, Haedi woke up to the ringing of a rooster's crow. The pumpkin had fallen out of the tree, her brother's bones were missing, and there amongst the chunks of orange meat, a giant black rooster proudly puffed up his feathers and crowed again. The sound resonated deep into Haedi's spirit.

She looked at the rooster closely. He was dark black with beautiful blue lacey patterns on his wings. His tail burst from his rump in a giant black, blue, and red display. He towered over Haedi.

She looked closely at the bird. She'd learned to be very, very afraid of birds. She was not afraid of this bird. Finally, he stopped crowing as the sun came up and, in the silence, Haedi spoke:

"Griffin is that you?" she asked.

He crowed one last time and tilted his head at her. She knew, somehow, the magic of this place had turned her brother into a bird. She ran to him and embraced his giant feathered neck, "I'm so glad you're alive!"

Once she was sure it was safe to leave, the two of them crossed through the thicket and left that nightmarish grove forever. Haedi hadn't wanted to take anything from the cursed place, but Griffin had insisted she raid the witches pantry. There they found a cache of magical seeds, foods that would grow even without the help of human intervention like irrigation and pesticide. He told Haedi that the seeds were a kind of precious treasure, and she had to take as many as she could carry. Hidden amongst the bags of seed, Haedi found a pendant that seemed to glow in the dark, it had a milky white surface that shimmered with blue and purple. She tucked it into her pocket.

She walked along thinking of how often she found herself traveling vast distances burdened by heavy loads and just as she was starting to feel sorry for herself, they came upon a massive pool of boiling hot volcanic water. It seemed to stretch for miles.

Haedi sat down feeling defeated. The distance was too far, and she was simply too tired. Griffin puffed up his feathers and then sat down beside her.

"You can't give up," he said to her, "everything you carry is precious, especially your spirit."

She looked at him and pain clouded her eyes, "I don't think I can walk another step." She looked down in shame. She knew people were depending on her and she failed.

"Then I'll carry you," he offered. He nodded reassuringly, "I've sat in the kennel while you worked and I've got magic, now. Let me carry you."

Haedi hesitated. She realized there was no choice and carefully she climbed onto his back.

Griffin didn't hesitate, as soon as she was holding on, he launched into the air. He was bolstered by magic and flew with a grace that no barnyard rooster ever had. They were partway across the pool when a massive jet of superheated water shot out from the center of the pool. A giant geyser that nearly pummeled them out of the sky. Deftly Griffin maneuvered around it. They landed safely on the far side of the pool and Haedi climbed down.

"That was awesome!" they said simultaneously, and both laughed.

"What do we do now?" Haedi asked her brother, "Should we go home?"

He looked at her, anger flashing in his eyes. He dug his talons into the ground and scratched angrily at the earth.

"No, I don't think we should go home. I think we should go after the Roc. I'm done living in fear."

Don't miss out!

Visit the website below and you can sign up to receive emails whenever Autumn Mist publishes a new book. There's no charge and no obligation.

https://books2read.com/r/B-A-VVXV-ZNREC

BOOKS 2 READ

Connecting independent readers to independent writers.

Also by Autumn Mist

The Bird Brain Books
This One's for the Birds
Carry On: Death Doulas of the Apocalypse
Unhatched Be: The Rise of Steampunk Portland
Hen's Teeth: Short Stories from the Bird Brain Books

Watch for more at www.autumnmistlit.com.

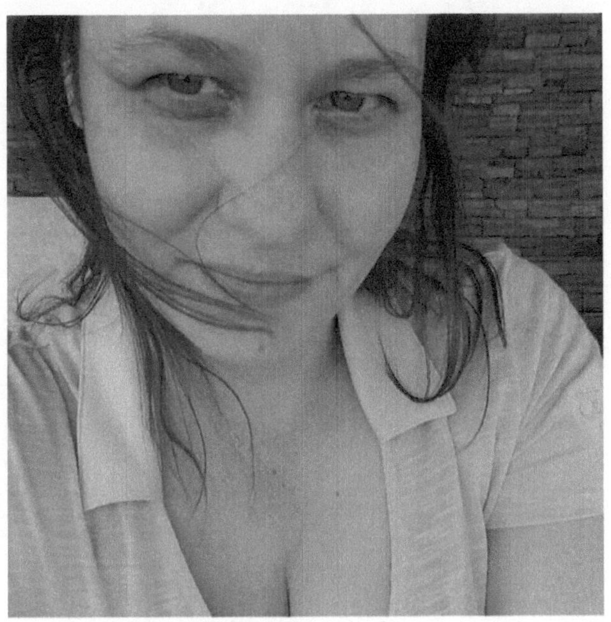

About the Author

I grew up reading novels like The Rats of Nimh, Momo, and My Side of the Mountain. My books are inspired by these tales that stretch the imagination, push us outside our comfort zone, and take us on a journey that is more than just miles.

I'm an anthropologist, writer and mother living in the misty hills of the oregon coast where I care for abandoned animals, spend many days rock hounding, and grow three beautiful children. Having seen the evils of humans from a young age, I learned to climb into books and out of my own skin. I write for the young people who understand life is hard and curling up with a good book can tend deep wounds. May these stories provide escape and solace to the reader.

Read more at www.autumnmistlit.com.